The Burdened Blood Series

Patronis

Written by: Caleb Barsness

Thanks for all the peppers. You need to teach me how grow a garden!! :)

Cale Barsness

Acknowledgements

To my beautiful wife Melissa Barsness, for being my inspiration and my rock-solid supporter. Your dedication to making our lives better every day was the driving force behind my decision to pursue my passion of writing.

To my beautiful children, Samuel Flint: I love how you are always asking questions to better understand the world around you. Your tender heart and observant attitude will take you far in this world.

Evelyn Shirlee: You are my little mother hen. You feel the need to make sure your older brother and younger sister are well taken care of. When you start something, you always strive to complete it. That attribute should help you succeed in the future.

Hadassah Jane: You are your father's clone! Sometimes when we are together it's like we can communicate without talking. You are the sweetest little girl I've ever met. Continue to just be yourself, no matter what anyone else says. I wish I would have taken that advice to heart many years ago.

To my grandparents: I am very thankful for all the stories you shared with me over the years and the wisdom you imparted to me. To my Grandpa Bass, who everyone says I am the spitting image of. I did not get much of a chance to know you, but from the stories I have heard, you were a fun-loving man who liked to collect things as a hobby. I've been able to catch short glimpses of you in old movies as you were an extra in many films.

To my Grandma Bass: I will always have the memories of coming and staying with you in California. The fun times we were able to share together have created a sort of nostalgia for me now that I am older.

To Gampee Barsness: Thank you for all the lessons and great love you showed to me over these many years. Your carefree attitude and friendly disposition always seemed to brighten my day. Thank you for being a second father to me.

To Gamee Barsness: Thank you for always opening your home to me. Your dedication to your family showed in every family event. Thank you for being a second mother to me as well.

I thank God for every moment he has given me with all of my grandparents.

Preface

You know, life is a lot like baseball. We all step up to the plate looking to hit the long fly, and life seems to throw us a steady diet of fastballs. We watch as they fly past us, and we hope to time our swing correctly so that we can drive one of those balls to the outfield. All we really want to do is be able to make our way around the base pads. But every so often life throws us a curve ball, and most people are frozen by it, unable to do anything but watch as it goes by. *My boy, the real success stories come from those who aren't caught looking in those situations. A real hero is a person who can hit the curve.* That was something that I remember Mr. Ambridge saying to me when we met for the first time over two years ago. I don't know why that stuck with me; I just remember thinking, *this guy really loves baseball!*

Brighton Bay Sanitarium
Assistant Warden Achiel Caldwell's Log
January 1st, 1949

Happy New Year! I am now three years removed from receiving my doctorate in Psychology and am in my second year as assistant warden at Brighton Bay Sanitarium in upstate Connecticut. Mr. Ambridge, the sanitarium warden, and my boss, said it was important to start a log. Seeing as it is a new year, I figured it would be the perfect time to begin my log. He said that it is key for any psychologist - so that all the daily patient interactions are recorded. That way one can look back on certain cases in the future to check for familiarity in patients' actions or similar behaviors among patients. Thus, I am starting this log with a bit about myself to see if maybe in the future I might look back at this first entry and have a good laugh.

My name is Achiel Byron Caldwell; I work at Brighton Bay Sanitarium. The property consists of roughly five acres situated about ten miles outside the town of Brighton, Connecticut. The grounds are quite lovely despite the purpose the sanitarium serves. There are abundant, lush trees, vibrant in the fall and bare and glistening in the winter. The facility itself is a three-story brick and mortar building. It has the basics of any larger establishment of its kind: a cafeteria, two sitting lounges, and a pool in the basement with men and women's washrooms on the main floor. There are enough rooms for 82 patients, with a staff of 15 nurses, 14 guardsmen, 6 doctors and a warden, many having their own small housing units on the grounds as well. Three cooks and a handy-man/janitor round out the team of state-paid employees. The sanitarium itself was built at the turn of the twentieth century and was intended to house only the rich degenerates. These families were willing to pay vast amounts of money for nurses and doctors to hide their family members, so their family name was not soiled. Later, in the thirties, the sanitarium ran low on patients and funds, so they signed an agreement with the State of Connecticut to take on any person the state deemed clinically insane, so long as there was room for them. For me, the building seemed to have an ominous look to it.

I went to college for my Doctorate of Psychology, but little did I know that once I was in the field I would come to dread the work. Although this job may sound intriguing, don't fool yourselves. Basically I write down and over-analyze the thoughts and ramblings of people who have been hurt so deeply that they choose not to live in the here and now, but rather hide their true selves behind an image that keeps them safe -- almost like a turtle that hides in its shell. That image, although shell-like for the user, usually portrays itself as "crazy" to the persons who interact with it. Most of the time these, "clinically insane" persons do not even know what the shell is doing. Thus, many of these people are sent to the sanitarium for safe keeping.

My job title also comes with sacrifice in certain areas. First, I am always kept very busy with my work, which means that I really don't have a life; a social one that is. Not to mention, my dwelling is also on the premises of the sanitarium, which makes it even harder for me to have any type of amusement or distraction. I am also a very bashful person. When I was well into my teen years my mother would always try to persuade me to go out with certain girls from my hometown, but they were never very keen on me. I wasn't considered particularly fun. I didn't play any sports. I was not particularly adept with the ladies, either. Now that I have this job title, it's as if I am even more of a misfit or outcast than I once deemed myself. I've been to the local dance hall in Brighton three or four times now and danced with some very beautiful women, but as soon as I tell them where I work, they look at me as though I've just grown two horns. I just figure that unless I change careers, I am bound to my work rather than to a wife for the rest of my life.

There is, however, a new nurse working at the sanitarium who has caught my eye. She has the most radiant brown hair; it almost shines in the sunlight that filters through the many windows in the cafeteria. Her eyes have a certain sparkle to them, and they are the first clue to her vibrant personality. The room simply lights up when she enters. She reports directly to Mrs. Kettler, the head nurse, so I have never had the opportunity to work with her. I've learned her name is Mattie Peranio. I was thinking about her as I walked home last night. In my

7

mind we were on first name terms, although I've never actually talked to her. It was New Year's Eve, and I thought of how much fun she must be having going into Brighton to celebrate, turning that beautiful smile on to everyone she sees. I wondered who the lucky chap would be who got to kiss her at midnight. I secretly wished it could be me, but I couldn't even bring myself to ask her out on a date. I can't take the rejection anymore. Lately if I do get out, I like to go see a movie; at least interesting things happen in the movies. I do wish that something exciting might happen to me in the future. I don't think I could go on with life as it is now.... working in this sanitarium until I am old and in need of help myself. Then at the end of my life the only legacy I will have produced would be this log book. I don't want to go to my grave not being remembered by anyone. This will be the last of my personal logs in this book.

Brighton Bay Sanitarium
Assistant Warden Achiel Caldwell's Log
April 8, 1949

I was alerted to a disturbance that occurred in the lunchroom at approximately half past eleven this morning. One patient stabbed another patient in the lower stomach, which started a small brawl and led to the death of the attacker. I was not present at the time, because I was in a meeting. The whole ordeal was explained to me by one of the security guards - Grant, who had been the closest and only sane witness to the event. Grant told me that I would not believe what had happened, but he wanted me to listen to his explanation until the end without interjecting. I promised him I would. He proceeded to tell me how he watched in disbelief as the man who was stabbed grabbed his attacker by the neck and yelled in a deep, other-worldly voice, "It is not my time!" He then threw his attacker twenty feet into the wall, where the attacker broke his neck and was killed instantly. He was right … I did not believe him, but Grant was the only true witness to what happened, so I had no other option than to take his word for it. Grant could identify both the attacker, George Barden, and the victim, Gabriel Patronis. Grant also mentioned how odd it was to hear that unearthly voice coming from Gabriel. Then the assistant explained that when the attacker was thrown up against the wall, it was almost as if he had been hit by some sort of force that had come from Patronis's hand. This sort of news was very unlikely, to say the least. I did not know where to go from here, seeing as Mr. Ambridge was on a sabbatical and would not return for another week. I went quickly left to confer with Mrs. Kettler and Mr. Trundle, to find out how to deal with this disturbance.

Gabriel Patronis was restrained, put in a straitjacket, and placed in solitary confinement after the event. The police were called and alerted to the incident. I had to write the incident report, and I made sure to omit the strange particulars. Then, I had to call Mr. Barden's relatives to inform them of his death. I quickly grabbed his file to locate his next of kin. I saw he only had one brother who lived in China. It would be a long time before he was alerted of this situation. Also in the file was a picture of the deceased man. He was a short fellow with rather stocky features. He had enormous forearms and very thick glasses. He did not look like the type to try to attack someone. In fact, he looked rather harmless. I found it difficult to pen the words that could express my regret for his brother's death and that it happened while I was acting as warden.

I was uncomfortable with the entire episode, so I decided to pull out Patronis's file. I discovered that Patronis had no birth certificate, no list of relatives, and only one incident on his criminal record. The only record that we had of him was for harassment charges, which he had received for harassing children in the local city library. The earliest record we had of him came from two years earlier. I thought it necessary to further my research, so I contacted the local police to see if I could get my hands on any records they might have on Patronis. I talked to

Cynthia, the woman in charge of civil records in Brighton, and she searched for Gabriel Patronis's file. The only thing she found was the actual police report from the harassment charge. It read as follows:

"We arrested Gabriel Patronis on February 17, 1949, in the Brighton Public Library. The defendant was accused of verbally harassing several young boys who were in the library. Ms. Carrigan, one of the librarians, said that she overheard Patronis yelling "You must know!" at several boys patronizing the library. She also said that she saw him follow them around the library.

He shadowed them from section to section until they finally left the library. The boys then went home and told their parents about the strange man. The parents filed a complaint with the police.' We also conducted a clean sweep through the library to check for any property that Patronis may have had. In the men's restroom, the police found a broken piece of mirror that was sharpened, suggesting use as a crude weapon of sorts. They also found an abundance of religious and mathematical writings inside one of the restroom stalls. Patronis admitted to having the weapon and to living in the library for the last several weeks. He also admitted to moving from library to library in the vicinity. This statement by Patronis makes sense, because there have been reports of disturbances from the public libraries in the surrounding area. Patronis was taken to the county jail and is awaiting trial for multiple charges of harassment and carrying a concealed weapon."

After finding this article I thought it necessary to speak to Patronis myself. I walked down to solitary confinement, where Patronis was being held. One guard was on duty outside the room. I asked the guard if he had ever seen the guilty man act out like this before. The guard responded that he had never acted out but rather walked around talking to himself in a whisper most of the time. He said Patronis was also a loner and liked to keep to himself. I looked in through the window and saw Patronis for the first time. He was wearing the straitjacket and had an ominous look about him. His blond hair was dreadlocked and hung down to his shoulders. He had a scraggly beard, which seemed to come to a point. His eyes were aqua blue and shown out of his sunken eye sockets like crystals, giving him an even more foreboding appearance, and under his eyes were bags that evidenced a lack of sleep. His mouth was scrunched up into a small smirk. I had the guard on duty open the door and usher me inside. As I entered I could hear Patronis humming a song as he bobbed his upper body back and forth. Patronis was sitting exactly in the center of the room. Below is the dialogue between Mr. Gabriel Patronis and me.

"Hello, Gabriel, my name is Dr. Caldwell."
There was a long pause. Patronis continued to hum.
"Do you know why you are here?" I asked him.
"I killed a man." He spoke in a monotone.
"Why did you kill this man?"

"He was an agent sent against me; he knew what I'm trying to do. He wanted to stop me from finishing my quest."

"What is this quest you speak of?" I was determined to get him to sort this out.

Patronis went back to humming with a big smile on his face.

"Are you not going to tell me?"

There was another long pause; Patronis was still humming the same tune, and to be honest, it was beginning to annoy me.

"Can you tell me why you were harassing those boys in the library back in February?'

"From the mouth of babes come the old stories. They can see this world in its true color; they can hear the earth turning." Was he trying to set me up in some kind of riddle?

Patronis paused at this and his eyes shifted slightly.

"They know where the evil ones creep about. They know who lurks in the shadows waiting to pounce. You think this safe house keeps me from harm, but wherever I go I am a target. I must go to where it is hidden and when I have it, the old ways will be stopped, and a new era will begin." Now I was intrigued in spite of myself.

"Gabriel, you won't be leaving. We are keeping you here because you need our help in caring for yourself."

"I don't need you!" He seemed to spit the words from his belly. "I'm biding my time until I find it... No, Dr. Caldwell, it is YOU who needs ME! This world is more savage than you could possibly imagine. You might say I am merely using you and your safe house until my time comes."

"Well.... oh, I see; you have something written on your arm ... may I see it?

Let's see, *'He will stand against the prince of princes'* Daniel 8:25 and *'he was given power over all kindred, tongues and nations'* Revelation 13:7."

'He was and is not and yet still is' Revelation 17:8."

A shiver went up my spine. "Where did you come from? Where is your family?"

Patronis leaned in close and whispered: "I don't exist and yet I am; I am a servant and yet belong to myself. I have no family ... I have no friends ... I have no place to rest my weary head..." I paused and thought about the statement.

"Do you remember anything from your past?" We had to start somewhere!

Patronis stared straight ahead as if in a trance, and then he whispered, "I can sense them sometimes you know. I feel their presence as if a black cloud were over my head. My hair stands on end and then ..." There was a pause and Patronis seemed to snap out of the fog he was in. "I'm finished with these formalities. I would show you the door, but I seem to be restrained and am prevented from showing you any courtesies."

I left that room feeling as if I had been the one who was being questioned. Feeling more confused than before I had arrived, I turned to leave but looked once more at the completely white, sterile room and the grinning man, also in white but now with a red stain making its way through the straitjacket. He was seated in the middle of the room.

Brighton Bay Sanitarium
Assistant Warden Achiel Caldwell's Log
April 9, 1949

I entered the sanitarium today quite early in the morning. Still perplexed, I wanted to have another talk with Gabriel Patronis. I managed to find out that at his trial on harassment charges, there were things that Patronis said things that caused the judge to question his sanity. He was then tested and deemed mentally insane and placed in Brighton Bay nearly four weeks ago.

When I came to the solitary confinement room in which Patronis was being held, I found the door wide open. I shut the sanitarium down immediately, sending all the patients to their rooms. I called the police and then sent my assistants to check the entire sanitarium to question all the caretakers thoroughly. One of the nurses found two of the patients who said they had seen Patronis the night before. They were immediately brought to my office where, presently, a few police officers stood around a map trying to figure out a search plan. The sanitarium was buzzing as nurses, guards, and policemen scoured the building and grounds, searching every possible spot on the premises that could be used by Patronis as a hiding place.

The two patients looked quite obviously guilty as they entered the room. The first to speak was one of the sanitarium's favorites, nicknamed "Cooties". Cooties was allowed more leeway at the sanitarium because of his outgoing attitude and good behavior. He was one of the few patients who was given particular jobs to pass his time. Cooties was walking back upstairs after his laundry duties were completed, and upon returning to his room late last night, he heard Gabriel calling to him. This of course is absurd, as solitary confinement rooms are completely sound-proof. Jones (Cooties' real last name was Jones) went to solitary confinement where he saw the guard had fallen asleep at his post. He went up to the cell where Patronis was being held. He said he opened the sliding door at bottom of the heavy iron door (usually used to push food or other objects into the room to keep from contacting the prisoner in any way). When Cooties put his hand inside the cell he felt Patronis's foot. Cooties said he had the other hand on the door itself and as he watched, the cell door became red. He got so scared he pulled his hand off and the door fell outward off its hinges, letting Gabriel out. The police seemed to think this story was nonsense, seeing as the sound of the door would have alerted the sleeping guard that the door had opened. I asked Cooties what happened after the door fell. He said that Gabriel emerged and told him that in return for releasing him his "mind would be renewed". All the while the guard never stirred from his slumber near the now-empty cell. Cooties, though kind, was not very bright.

Allen, the guard on duty at the time, tried to defend himself, "That's impossible! That door was locked and bolted shut. Cooties could never have gotten in there." You could see there was wild disbelief mixed with shame in his old eyes. He seemed to know that this incident would snuff out his rather cushy job.

The other patient, Sarah Tralton, had a speech impediment, making it almost impossible to understand her. The nurses and I had to do our best to read between the lines of her account. After multiple attempts and over an hour later, the gist was that Gabriel entered her room while she was sleeping and told her to remove his straitjacket. She did as he ordered and then opened her window for him. He promised her the same miracle he had promised Cooties if she would help him.

There were several holes in their stories. In order for Cooties to get the door open, he would have had to have the key to open the steel lock on the door. A group of us went to examine the door for evidence. We noticed that the lock on the door had been melted off. The odor of burnt metal brought involuntary tears to my eyes. This meant that an immense amount of heat would have been used in order to melt the steel bolts that held the door in place. This in turn would have killed both Jones and Mr. Patronis! It was truly unbelievable, yet the lock was still hot to the touch.

The problem with Ms. Tralton's story was similar in nature. The windows at the sanitarium have iron bars on the inside and outside. Furthermore, Ms. Tralton would have needed a key to remove the straitjacket on Patronis's upper body. When the group went to check the window, we found that both the inside and the outside iron bars, like the lock on Patronis' cell, had melted away. The inside bars lay on the floor in Ms. Tralton's room. The bars were so hot that they had burned marks into the tiled floor. Right next to the bars laid the straitjacket; it looked as if the straps had been cut clean through with scissors. Again, all the iron materials were too hot to touch. Ms. Tralton's room was on the third floor, which meant Patronis would have had to jump. The window looked to be at least ten feet off the ground. Below the window at ground level sat a large grouping of black cap bushes. They grew three feet high and were three feet in width out from the walls of the sanitarium. Patronis would have had to jump a long way out if he wanted to clear the heavy thorns on these bushes. It seemed unlikely that Gabriel could have avoided the bushes, so I sent two policemen down to check for any signs of disturbance or a blood trail. They came back saying that there was no sign of shrubbery being disturbed and no sort of trail leading away from the area.

Gabriel had walked out of the sanitarium with nothing preventing his escape. The police set up roadblocks on all the surrounding area roadways. My assistant set up search parties in the nearby woods. A few more officers and I visited the nearby towns looking for any sign of

Gabriel. Our search proved futile, and later that night the reality of the situation loomed upon us .... Gabriel Patronis had left no evidence of a trail.

A report went out that evening on the radio:
"Yesterday at approximately 10:00 p.m., a patient from the Brighton Bay Sanitarium escaped the grounds. All people in the surrounding towns should be on the lookout for Gabriel Patronis, a six-foot-tall, white male with blond dreadlocks. He also has tattoos on his neck, arms and chest. This man is very dangerous and could be armed. If you happen to see a man answering to this description, go indoors and call the police immediately. Make no attempt to stop him on your own. Once again, this warning is for all residents of the towns surrounding Brighton Bay Sanitarium."

Brighton Bay Sanitarium
Assistant Warden Achiel Caldwell's Log
April 11, 1949

Police received a tip that there was a strange man fitting the description of Gabriel seen at Mickey's Bookshop yesterday. Mickey had also gone missing, and his store had been locked up since yesterday morning. Several officers and I went to said bookshop around seven o'clock in the evening. No one was around when the police broke down the front door, weapons readied. We instantly started a search of the bookstore. One of the policemen walked over and opened the door to the hall closet, and there he found a wide-eyed and terrified Mickey. He was bound rather crudely with packing tape, and his mouth taped in a similar fashion. One officer radioed for a crime unit to join them, as another officer released Mickey and instantly started to bombard him with a barrage of questions.

By then the lights had been turned on and all but a couple of policemen had crowded around poor Mickey. A handful of other officers and I began to walk down the book aisles, looking for anything, really, and yet nothing in particular. I came to the history section and let my eyes quickly take in the titles on the weathered bindings. It was then that I noticed the piece of paper sticking out from in-between two of the books. I would not have given it a thought except that the paper had my name on it. I took it out and opened it. There were just five lines scribbled in a hurry:

"Killers walk amongst,
Seekers by air,
Keepers by the sea,
Finders underground,
Minders never free."

I instantly thought that this could be a clue for the police, but then I remembered we were chasing a clinically insane man, and these five lines were probably just the mindless scribbling of a madman. The fact that the message had my name on it also had me guarded. I slipped the note into my pocket.

When I went back up to the front of the store, Mickey was explaining how a crazed looking individual came into his store and began to run up and down the aisles looking for something. Mickey had yelled at him to get out, which had made the man angry. He knocked Mickey on the head with a rather large book and then taped him up and placed him in the broom closet.

The police then reasoned that the man was Patronis, that he took the keys and locked the front door, turned the sign around to the 'closed' position and left by way of the back exit. It was later determined that Patronis had been looking for clothing, and had in fact found a spare pair of clothes Mickey kept in a storage room in back. The dresser in which said clothes were kept was disturbed and the contents left in a haphazard manner. As the police continued sweeping the bookstore for more evidence, I returned to the sanitarium for the day.

After retiring to my quarters later that night, I started to change into my pajamas suddenly I remembered the piece of paper I had found in the bookstore. I took it out of my pocket and held the folded paper in my hand. I instantly felt a wave of guilt for keeping the verse from the police, as it was so obviously a piece of evidence. I slowly unfolded the paper and read the lines again:

"Killers walk amongst,
Seekers by air,
Keepers by the sea,
Finders underground,
Minders never free."

A faint memory started taking shape in my mind. I had heard this once before, or something vaguely similar, but I could not remember where. I sat there searching my memory and decided to get a better look at the slip of paper. I put the paper up to a lamp in my room and immediately noticed something. There was more writing on the paper! It had been folded when I found it, so I had unfolded it and looked at the inside. But on the other side, where my name was printed there was more writing.
The paper had five more words on it:

The Legends of Green Eagle

Then it came to me! My grandmother used to read to me from *The Legends of Green Eagle*. They were old Indian tales told to amuse children. I hadn't heard these stories in years. The book was one of the few things my parents had given me when Grandma had passed away.

My mother told me around the time I turned seventeen that my grandmother made it clear she wanted me to have the book of tales. Not much interest in reading fables for children, I tossed it onto my shelf without much more thought.

What could Patronis have wanted with this book? I went to my bookshelf, and among all my Psychology, Anatomy, and Science textbooks I found a small, green leather-bound book that once belonged to my grandmother. I pulled it out and stared at it momentarily. Realizing as I looked it over that I had never even so much as glanced at the book since owning it, I opened to the inner cover and saw a note written in my grandmother's writing. I could hardly believe my eyes when there was the mysterious five-lined poem that Patronis had written on the scrap of paper. Underneath it was a sentiment from my grandmother.

"To my happy little grandson, Achiel
This book may help you see the world in a different light.
Lovingly, Grandma Ruth"

I collapsed into my chair, perplexed and exhausted, yet slightly excited. I couldn't believe how preposterous this all was, and yet it had strings of sanity woven throughout. I decided to open the book and read.

The Legends of Green Eagle
Interpreted by: Benito Cajero
Told by: Ta'awa Hotsko
Calabre I

There once lived a man of great ability. Although he was well known, he was
driven out by his own people, for he had slain his own brother. The man traveled far and wide trying to find a home. He was forced to hunt and gather food to survive. He moved from place to place, hating to be alone yet scorned by everyone who saw him. He traveled for many moons until he came to a spot where the sun was hot and the land was filled with wildlife. It was here that the man decided to lie down and die. But before he could enter the spirit world, a voice called out to him: "Why do you wish to end your life at such a time as this?"

The man answered, "I have nowhere to go, no land to call my own, and no people to care for." The voice called down again, "I shall grant you this land and I will provide for you the companions you desire. All you must do is choose four different animals you wish to serve your needs." The man rejoiced in the favor he had found with this being and asked, "What can I call you?" The voice answered: "I am Quomvi Ta'aho, I will be your guardian and you shall find me when you call upon me. I shall make your name great and the people that come after you will remember you to the end of their days." The man was very grateful for this gift but he asked, "What must I do to be given these gifts?"

The voice answered: "You must listen to me and do as I command when the time comes." Thus, the man went in search of the creatures that would usher him into his kingdom.

Brighton Bay Sanitarium
Assistant Warden Achiel Caldwell's Log
April 12, 1949

Sleep eluded me last night. As quickly as eight o'clock could arrive, and being so conveniently a Saturday, I hopped in my car and drove to Brighton to visit Mickey at the bookstore. He was just opening up when I got there. I immediately entered and found Mickey organizing a stack of books. I had also brought my own copy of *The Legends of Green Eagle* and reassuringly patted my pocket where it was tucked away. I nodded and asked Mickey how he was doing after the rather exciting, albeit frightening, events that had taken place in his store.

Mickey told me he was fine, just a bit shook up and slightly sore from being taped up and held in his broom closet. He considered himself fortunate as the police found him rather quickly. It was then that I placed my leather-bound book on the counter in front of Mickey. I can't be sure, but his eyes seemed to have widened ever so slightly.

I asked Mickey if he could tell me the origin of the book.

He picked up the volume and glanced through it. "Well, let me see..." he said thoughtfully as he peering over his glasses.

"Ah... *The Legends of Green Eagle*. These are fables written by Padre Benito Cajero. He heard the tales when visiting the Hopi Tewa Indians in 1703. He was setting up a church near the Pueblo villages of these Native American people. He learned their language and then proceeded to learn about their culture. These fables were told by an old medicine man. The tribe revered him as sacred, and he lived alone at the top of the village mountain. However, every day he would ride his donkey down into the village and gather the children together to tell them all these stories. Deeply intrigued by the stories, Cajero wrote them down. Actually, there are five books that make up *The Legends of Green Eagle*; one for each season and the fifth was used for special astronomical events such as a meteor shower, an eclipse or a blood moon. The books are: Calabre for winter, Melisandric for fall, Bobothan for summer and Fuerdith for spring. The special book was named the Coakidren. Some say that Cajero never did hear all of the stories from this book. They have been forgotten over time and in fact, there are only about 1000 copies of this book left in circulation today. This one looks to be from the 1870's."

Mickey paused and looked up at me. "You wouldn't be willing to part with it, would you? You can see," he motioned around his store, "I'm a collector of antique books, and this would be a great addition to the…"

I cut him off and asked if these stories were believed to be true or if they were in fact simply fables, legends and stories written and passed on to learn from in a parable-like manner.

Mickey scratched his head. "Hmm? Oh no, they aren't real; they're just another form of fairy tales, that is all. Are you all right, Dr. Caldwell? You don't look so well."

I was starting to feel rather flushed and decided to head back to the sanitarium.
I said thank you and goodbye when Mickey blurted out, "How about I give you $10.00 for the book?" Rather surprised and unsure as to what to say next, I turned and thanked him but told him but emphasized I was not interested in selling at this time. He continued to press me.

"How about Twenty?"

At this point I was all the more confused. "Don't you already have a copy of this book, Mickey?"

He cleared his throat rather nervously and said, "Well, yes I do, but it's not an antique; in fact, it's only a couple of years old. They just printed about 100 copies in 1940. How about Fifty? It's my last offer."

I glanced down at the book in my hand and told Mickey as kindly as possible that the book was a family heirloom and was not for sale. I was about to turn again and try to exit the bookstore, when Mickey raised his voice slightly. It caused me to turn yet again and focus my attention on the bookkeeper.

"Wait a minute…. that guy yesterday - the one who locked me in the closet - he was mumbling the lines of that book. Yes, I remember now, 'Killers walk amongst, Seekers by air, Keepers by the sea, Finders underground, Minders never free.' He must have said it like thirty times. What gives, Achiel? What are you up to?"

I told him that I was merely trying to better understand the mind and motives of my patient.

I briskly left the book shop with the information I had been after, but the puzzle remained.
What was Gabriel looking for and why did he want this book? I went back to the sanitarium and looked in on some patients. I tried to clear my mind of this nonsense, but it kept creeping back into the corners of my mind. I couldn't focus on lunch, despite my ravenous appetite, so I decided to take a walk around the sanitarium gardens. The air still smelled of winter, but there was also the smell of awakening earth and a hint of rain. For the first time that day, I was able to think of other things. I told

myself that the police could handle the situation and that I should return to my duties. Most weekends I would be free to do as I liked because I was only assistant warden, but this weekend, things were different: I was acting warden. It was time to get back to doing what I was being paid to do. So after lunch I went back and met with the head nurse, Mrs. Kettler, who informed me everything was going well, despite yesterday's events. I got the same report from the head of security, Mr. Trundle, saying that Mr. Mayfield (the janitor/handyman) had re-welded the bars to Ms. Tralton's windows, and put a new lock system on the door to solitary confinement. Trundle also noted that he would personally order two new straitjackets come Monday morning. After those meetings were over I settled into Mr. Ambridge's desk and took a first look at the mail that had been piling up for the past four days. Mr. Ambridge had given me strict instructions to open only certain mail, mostly just the bills, and perhaps any roaming promotional sales jargon that would be considered trash. I skimmed through the lot, pulling out three bills, two promotions for a vacuum cleaner and a typewriter. Near the bottom I found a piece of personal mail. The outside said, "To Whom It May Concern". Being the inquisitive man that I am, I ripped open the letter. It read:

To Whom It May Concern,
I have recently been informed that you have a tenant living with you now who goes by the name of Gabriel Patronis. This man is of great importance to me and my work here in Arizona. I would greatly appreciate a

meeting with you or someone on your staff, preferably a meeting in person. Seeing as I am an invalid, I would be willing to pay for you or your staffer to come and meet with me here at my residence. Please respond to this letter as soon as you're able, as the urgency of Gabriel to my work is critical.

Thank you for your time,
Draxman Pista

The letter brought back a swell of emotions as I rushed head long into more theories and thoughts about the Patronis case. Is this where Gabriel was headed? There was no way to escape this mystery, nowhere to hide from the clues. They were all around, encircling me like a web; and as soon as I calmed my mind and cleared myself of one sticky thread, another clue took its place until; finally, I would have no choice but to try and solve the mystery myself. I couldn't stand it anymore. I had to go home; but just as I put on my coat and grabbed the letter from off the desk, the phone rang. Not thinking straight, I picked up the phone and said hello.

"Hello, Edward, it's me, Mickey. Say, you might have a problem on your hands. That mad man from yesterday? Patronis? Well, he stole one of my books - *The Legends of Green Eagle*"

"Oh," I said, trying my best to sound like Ambridge. "Is that all?"

30

"That isn't even half of it. Your understudy came to see me today. I know him well - he's been in a bunch of times to buy books and sell me some of his textbooks. We've talked an awful lot about the sanitarium. Anyway, he comes in this morning and has that same book - only an older copy of it - and starts asking me questions about it. I think you might need to talk to that young man. Now hear me out here, because this is going to sound insane, but I think he is in cahoots with Patronis. Heck, he might have been the person who let Patronis out last night."

I was silent on the other end of the phone; I could feel myself getting very hot, and a bead of cold sweat ran down my brow.

"How else can you explain them having the same book? I tell you, something just doesn't add up about the situation, Warden. Anyway, I think you should at least have a talk with the boy and see what he was doing last night, that's all."

"Well, I will talk to him later next week... he's off for the weekend; besides, I trust that boy more than you could ever know. He doesn't seem like the type to help a madman escape. It's probably just a coincidence, Mickey."

"Well, you talk to him, at least do that. I don't want any more of those crazies coming into my bookstore!"

"All right, Mickey! Goodnight." I think he bought the ruse.

After I hung up the phone, I immediately grabbed the letter I had opened and the note I had found in Mickey's bookstore, and put them in my copy of the *The Legends of Green Eagle*. I rushed out of Ambridge's office and back to my quarters. It was dark now, and there were only a few lights left on in the place. On my way out I noticed a dorm door had been flung open and the light was shining from inside. I went to shut the door, but when I got there, I realized the significance of the room: it was the dorm Patronis had stayed in prior to being placed in solitary confinement. The police had not searched the room because they had only been told that Patronis was being kept on the solitary hall, which was on a completely different floor. I briskly entered the small space and scanned the room carefully for any sign of something amiss. The room had a bed, a bed pan, and a sitting chair with a lamp behind it. There was a shelf holding a few books, a dresser and a table with nothing on it. I ripped open all the dresser drawers, sending their contents onto the bare floor. There was nothing of significance, just a bunch of regulation sanitarium clothing. I then went to the bookshelf where four books were within easy reach on the bottom shelf. The first book was **Peter Pan.** I looked through it but found nothing. The second and third books: *A Princess of Mars* and **Heart of Darkness** revealed the same disappointment. But the fourth book was a **Bible**. And as

I opened and thumbed through it I found one passage had been highlighted:

Genesis 4:10-15
"The Lord said, "What have you done? Listen! Your brother's blood cries out for me from the ground. Now you are under a curse and driven from the ground, which opened its mouth to receive your brother's blood from your hand. When you work the ground, it will no longer yield its crops for you. You will be a restless wanderer on the earth."

Cain said to the Lord, "My punishment is more than I can bear. Today you are driving me from the land, and I will be a restless wanderer on the earth, and whoever finds me will kill me."

But the Lord said to him, "Not so; anyone who kills Cain will suffer vengeance seven times over." Then the Lord put a mark on Cain so that no one who found him would kill him.

It really did not make much sense to me, so I continued my search. I studied the walls again, this time more closely, but there was nothing. Somewhat disappointed, I sat in the armchair. It was then I noticed something peeking out from underneath the bed; it was a red line. I got down on my hands and knees and looked under the bed. Then I got up and shoved the bed away from the corner. There on the wall was a bunch of poorly etched writings, along with a few pictures. All the writing and drawings had been written in smeared blood. There was a five-lined poem and beneath it was written:

"All clamoring for the eternal prize.
Look high, look low - for what ye seek lays hidden;
stained by the history of demise.
Sin and shame cloud its past,
but the prize shall be found and destroyed at last."

A crude map had been drawn beneath the poem with a dotted line traveling from what looked to be Canada down through the east coast. Far below that an "X" was drawn in the middle of what appeared to be Mexico.

Perhaps the most chilling thing I found was on the other wall. Etched there was a rudimentary diagram of four creatures that looked like they belonged on the walls of a cave instead of on the walls of a bedroom. It was drawn in quadrant style with lines separating each picture. On the top right was the picture of a man's head connected to the body of a bird; under the picture was the word "Strix". On the top to the left, was a picture of something most closely resembling a reptile or lizard, at least its head, but it had the body of a man with a long tail protruding from behind. The words "Insignem Soparli" were written to describe the odd image. Below the reptile man was the word "Sapator" and under the word was a picture of what looked like a rodent with very muscular human forearms. Finally, to the right of that picture was an image of a merman. It was the only picture in the group I recognized. Above the picture was the word "Syreni". That concluded the treasure trove of information that I found under Patronis's bed. I don't know how long I was staring at that diagram, but what took me out of my trance was an unfamiliar voice from behind me. "He took my birthday money." Startled, I turned and in the door frame stood Sarah Tralton. My whole face went numb and my jaw dropped. It was the first time in four years that Sarah had spoken a complete sentence. Not only that, Sarah always seemed to have a glazed look on her face. But as she stood there however, her eyes were trained on me. "I had over $50.00 from my parents in my dresser, and he took it. I'm sure of that." It was anything but normal behavior from her. But there was no time. I calmly told her to return to her room, and I ran to call the police.

Brighton Bay Sanitarium
Assistant Warden Achiel Caldwell's Log
April 13, 1949

Today I called to inform Mr. Ambridge of the twists and turns of the last week. He said he was going to cut his sabbatical short. I think he knew there would be many questions to answer from the public. The City of Brighton would hold city council meetings and the mob would voice their disdain for the sanitarium. Ambridge would have to calm them all down with apologies and promises. Then he would bring paperwork on the few patients who had been "cured" and returned to civilian life. He would present evidence to the city council members that the sanitarium's work had a worthwhile cause. I had been present at one of these meetings before and very likely this one would not be the last either. The only reason the sanitarium had not been shut down was because of Ambridge. Edward's tactics were two-fold; first, he would always come up with a plan to further the fortifications that surrounded the sanitarium. In addition, he gave a generous amount of money to the city every year to help renovate the growing neighborhoods. Ambridge was a well-known doctor and his research manuscripts sold many thousands of copies so it was not hard for him to shell out some of his earnings in order to keep the people in Brighton happy. After hearing an Ambridge speech, the city council members would soothe the angry citizens and send them back to their homes. I on the other hand, was not looking forward to another one of these witch hunts. My mind was churning as I tried to figure a way to get out of this meeting. I figured I could maybe remove myself by reviewing the case files of a few patients. In this situation, it might be best to review the files of Tralton and Jones, because of their recent misadventures with Patronis. The only question was whether their reviews would be considered important enough to get me away from all the madness.

Brighton Bay Sanitarium
Assistant Warden Achiel Caldwell's Log
April 14, 1949

Ambridge was back today, and with his return all of Brighton seemed to surround Brighton Bay. Reporters were congregating outside the gates, and the sheriff and three of his deputies were in Ambridge's office when I first stopped by at ten o'clock in the morning. Ambridge looked like he hadn't slept in a couple of days. When he saw me, he called me over.

"I'm just about to go into a meeting, Achiel, so I'm going to need you to be in charge again for just a little bit."

"Is there something wrong again?" Of course I was concerned.

"It seems that Patronis is causing problems wherever he goes. I'll give you more details later, as I'm going to call a short staff meeting later tonight."

With that, Ambridge, the sheriff and the other law enforcement officials went down the hall to meet in the library. I stayed in Ambridge's office. I thought that this meeting might be to figure out a forward plan with the police department to keep the peace with the citizens of Brighton. The hours seemed to drag the rest of the day. I did my usual rounds and met with both Kettler and Trundle separately. It seemed as if the sanitarium was returning to its normal everyday routine. Other than the escape of Gabriel Patronis, my life would still be normal. His disappearance allowed me to break out of my regular scheduled grind. Even though I was physically quite tired, I felt somewhat emotionally rejuvenated. Almost as if I were a detective solving a case rather than a sanitarium employee.

At six o'clock that evening I was called into the library, where Ambridge and the sheriff still convened. Trundle and Kettler followed me in. The only other person in the room stood like a tall statue over in the far corner. He was a head above six feet tall, bald and had a large, flat nose that covered a good portion of his face. The man was wearing a black hooded cloak over a simple button-up shirt and trousers. But his most distinctive feature was his beady green eyes. They were an emerald color the likes of which I had never seen before. They seemed to gleam out from underneath the hood he wore. The mood seemed tense; the air seemed electrically charged. The ash tray on the coffee table was overflowing with spent cigarettes and cigars. They had smoked so much that there were clouds of smoke blocking our view of the upper level of the library. Mr. Ambridge cleared his throat in order to start the meeting.

"I've called you all here to explain what our plan needs to be going forward." Ambridge was all business. "We have a rough road I fear, but if we stick to the plan that Sheriff MacKenzie and I have worked out, we should be fine."

Sheriff MacKenzie interjected, "Perhaps you should tell them what happened in Pittsburgh, Edward."

"That's right. It appears that Mr. Patronis is more dangerous than I thought. Three days ago, there were multiple witnesses who claim they saw someone who fit the description of Patronis. He was fighting with five other individuals in an alleyway near a bus stop. Three of the other men who were in the altercation are in serious condition in a local hospital, and another man was killed. The fifth man ran away before the police could question him. As for Patronis, witnesses say he boarded another bus heading south long before police arrived. The Pittsburgh police put a patrol-man at every bus station within a 50-mile radius of the Pittsburgh area."

"They never found anyone answering the description of our madman. I could have guessed as much," MacKenzie admitted in a grim tone.

"So what is our plan of action going forward?" asked Trundle.

"Well, I've given it a lot of thought," Ambridge responded, "because Patronis is still supposed to be under our care and supervision, it is our duty to try to find him and bring him back. Meanwhile, we also need to be looking to reestablish our rapport with the people of Brighton.

Trundle was more than troubled. "Are you suggesting that someone from the sanitarium should go after Gabriel? That is madness; no one in their right mind is going to volunteer to go after that man."

"Who said anything about volunteering? I have selected a person I think would be perfect for the job. Before I go too much further I must explain the presence of Mr. Dicere. This gentleman was sent by a wealthy businessman named Draxman Pista, who claims to be Patronis's manager. Mr. Dicere says that Pista has been out of sorts since Patronis left his residence over two years ago. What's even more disturbing is that Gabriel left no note or showed any signs of being discontented; rather, he just up and left one day. Since then, Pista has spent countless hours and a large amount of money trying to find Gabriel, and now that he has discovered he was a resident at Brighton Bay and has escaped, he is willing to help. Dicere says that Pista is more than willing to fund a team to search for Mr. Patronis. His only demand is that as soon as Gabriel is found, he be returned to Pista unharmed and with the proper paperwork necessary to keep Patronis in his care."

Dicere further explained, "Mr. Pista stresses the urgency of this mission. Patronis is vital to the work that Pista is doing."

"Do you mind if we ask what kind of work that is?" Kettler interjected.

Shifting a bit in his seat, Dicere explained, "To that end I am unable to answer your question, other than to say that the work Pista is doing is for the government and is highly classified."

"So I'm guessing you want to send me on this mission, eh Edward?" Trundle almost puffed out his chest.

"Actually, I need you here for support with our meeting coming up in Brighton. The same goes for you, Mrs. Kettler."

Kettler wanted to know, "Then who are you sending on this wild goose chase?"
"I am going to send Caldwell after Gabriel."

Shocked, I almost sputtered, "Me? Why me? I'm not trained for this sort of thing!"

"Calm down Achiel! You will have a team of people with you. Besides, I think this might look very good on your resume. It will be your chance to work on your leadership skills. In addition, you know the most about Patronis;

I've seen that you were looking at his file. Mickey told me you were in questioning him about Patronis too."

I blushed quickly at the mention of Mickey, Hopefully Ambridge believed in me more than the theories of a day-dreaming bookstore owner

"You will have one of my most trusted officers by your side as well, Mr. Caldwell," MacKenzie added.

"Mr. Trundle, can you spare a guard to accompany Achiel?"

"Yes, I suppose I can send Grant along."

"How about you, Mrs. Kettler, can you afford to lose a nurse for a few weeks?"

"The only nurse I can give you is Ms. Peranio." Everyone seemed to be guarding his or her own importance.

Mr. Pista has also sent his personal bodyguard to assist you. His name is Custos Tenebris." My team seemed complete.

"So Dr. Caldwell, you have your team now. You will need to leave soon. Mr. Patronis is already several days ahead of you."

"Pardon me, sir, but we don't even have a clue of where Patronis was going," I felt I had to point out what seemed obvious to me.

Mr. Pista sent strict instructions to bring you to his villa in Arizona. From there, we all can form a plan of action."

"I suggest that we inform the other people going on this trip that they should start packing. I want them to be at the train station in Brighton tomorrow morning" Ambridge was back to practicalities.

With the meeting concluded, everyone scurried off to inform their respective chess pieces. I was left in the room with Ambridge and Dicere. I moved over to Ambridge and attempted to quietly speak my fears and doubts to him. "Mr. Ambridge, are you sure that you want me to lead this group? Wouldn't MacKenzie or Trundle be a better choice for this job?"

Dr. Ambridge studied the books on a certain shelf as he contemplated the question. Then he spoke. "I have considered all my options, and I have given this decision my full attention for the past two days. I believe you have the most experience with this man. I heard you even went to talk to him when he was in solitary confinement. I think you are the best option available to me. Not to mention, MacKenzie has his own work he must do, and Trundle is of greater help to me if he stays here. I need him in order to sort out all the issues of the sanitarium, so events like those that transpired recently will never happen again. I am putting all my trust in this mission, son. This next week at the meetings in Brighton I'm going to promise the people that we will get Patronis back so he can answer for the crimes he's committed. That means you return with Patronis or don't bother coming back at all."

I was aghast. "You can't say that, Doctor. You know our efforts to catch Patronis are most likely futile at best." Ambridge didn't budge from his position. "I have no other choice, Achiel. This type of thing has happened too many times in the past. MacKenzie says if I don't make this case, the city council will likely call for my resignation and shut down the sanitarium altogether."

There was a pause after he spoke, and he turned away from me to look at the books behind his desk. I knew what he was thinking: He did not have much faith in this plan, but he did not really have a choice. He knew that ultimately his career was coming to a quick end. Almost in a whisper he continued, "Go and ready yourself, Achiel, and know that my thoughts and prayers will be with you."

I walked out of the room in somewhat of a stupor. My mind could not wrap itself around what had just happened. I think part of my problem was that deep down I was afraid of Gabriel Patronis; he was unpredictable, and some of the things he did while here at the sanitarium seemed to be almost unearthly in nature. The other feeling that seemed to be bubbling up inside me was pure sadness for Doctor Ambridge. I would be leaving the sanitarium for more than a couple of hours for the first time in over three years. In fact, there was a chance that after tomorrow, I would be leaving Brighton Bay for good.

Brighton Bay Sanitarium
Assistant Warden Achiel Caldwell's Log
April 15, 1949

Today saw the start of our journey. We all gathered at the Brighton Train Station at six o'clock in the morning. I was filled with nerves, but mostly excited. I met the other people in my party. Mr. Benson, the policeman, is in his late thirties and has thinning hair and a very bulbous-looking nose that clashes with his box-like head. He stands at about five feet, eight inches, and has the most amazing blonde mustache I have ever seen. His blue eyes show signs of agitation and disbelief. He has a rather pudgy middle that seems to jut out over his belt. In contrast, the man named Custos towers over everyone, even Dicere. The two look very similar otherwise. Custos wore the same style of clothing with the black cloak and plain shirt and trousers of a dark brown color. They both had the same facial features with that eerie eye color and the nose that seemed to cover too much of their faces. But the big difference between the two came in bulk. Custos was broad, both in shoulders and in legs; he was quite the physical specimen. The others I knew from previously working together. We boarded the train and were shown to our cabins. I was to share a cabin with Grant, the security officer from Brighton Bay. Donald Grant was a charmer. I cannot tell you how many times he's told me a tale of his escapades in Brighton. He seemed to get around quite nicely. He was your typical tall, dark and handsome, and he played that card well. As we unpacked our luggage in our small cabin, he began to converse with me.

"They say you're the ringleader of this little circus. Is that true?" He looked at me with his deep brown eyes. "I am, I mean," I was almost stuttering. "Mr. Ambridge thought it appropriate to put me in charge of the group," I answered. He continued unpacking for a few moments and then he responded, "Well, this should be fun. Let me tell you though, if I get my hands on Patronis, you won't be bringing him back to this Pista guy." With that he walked out of the cabin, leaving me with a sick feeling in my stomach. There were already signs of mutiny before our trip had even gotten underway. How would these people view me? Would they ever listen to me?

We all met again in the sitting car, and there Dicere handed out envelopes with our meal stipends for the train. A lot of eyebrows were raised at the $75.00 we were given. It seemed very generous seeing as a sandwich and fries was only 65 cents. Obviously, Pista was a wealthy man indeed. The train we were riding was a Deluxe Streamliner. Pista had already paid for our passage as well. We were in some of the deluxe cabins near the front of the train. The train also had two sitting cars, an observatory car that had a glass ceiling and three different eating cars. One was set up like a diner, the second was a fancy Italian restaurant and the third was a bar that served drinks and sandwiches. The train was quite nice, and I spent the rest of the day exploring it. That night I went in to look at the game room, where in one corner a chess board was set up. I went over to have a little self-duel to see which half of my brain might win the upper hand (psychologist joke). At some point Benson and Grant sat at a table behind me, but I did not know they were there until they began to talk:

Grant spoke first. "So what do you think of this whole plot? I mean, I only found out I was going on this trip yesterday."

"It was similar with me," Benson responded. "I was told to 'pack enough clothes for two weeks and be ready to leave for the train station at 5:15 a.m. tomorrow. By the way, you're headed to Arizona, so pack accordingly."

Grant nodded and asked, "Did you know anything about this whole thing before they told you about the mission yesterday?"

"I have been in on this case from the start. This guy Patronis is all sorts of crazy! When we arrested him in the library, we found some weird writing he had done in one of the stalls of the men's bathroom. He had no wallet on him; in fact, the only piece of identification we found on the guy was a library card. Some old librarian probably had pity on him and issued him one so he could check out books if he pleased."

"I didn't think you had to check books out if you lived in the library itself." Grant wasn't the only one confused.

"How did the guy live in there without ever being noticed?"

"He told us he had been moving from library to library, trying not to get caught. I guess when he came to the Brighton library he found that the janitor had put up an 'Out of Service' sign on the door of one of the stalls in the men's restroom. The janitor went two weeks without cleaning that stall, which happened to be exactly how long Patronis had been living at the library."

"What were the writings like - were they even legible?" Grant asked.

"They were... otherworldly," Benson was thinking out loud. "I have never seen anything like them in my entire life. It wasn't just writing either; there were pictures that appeared to be very similar to hieroglyphics, you know, the writings the Egyptians employed. Anyway, it all seemed to stem outward, almost like a plant from a seed. The one thing it all centered around was a five-line poem."

"Do you remember what it said?"

Benson: "Yeah... it kind of burned in my memory 'Killers walk amongst, Seekers by air, Keepers by the sea, Finders underground, Minders never free.' The funny thing is when we got the call from Brighton Bay, I found the same type of drawings on the walls of Patronis's cell."

I had the goose bumps. I thought perhaps Gabriel was crazy and those confounding drawings had come from his deranged psyche. But now I knew better. Gabriel was searching for something; his drawings were like a mathematical web bringing him ever closer to the final equation. Could he possibly have gone in search of the answer already? Were we too late to apprehend him now? I came back from my concentrated thinking and found that Benson and Grant were still talking. But this time I realized that they did not know I was behind them.

"What do you think about that pip-squeak they put in charge of this whole rescue mission? He's no more fit to lead this group then Patronis himself."

It was obvious that Benson agreed with Grant's appraisal of my abilities.

"He seems to me like a regular Bonaparte, if you know what I mean. A little too big for his britches. Let me tell you, if he makes one false move during this operation, I'll be taking over."

"I'd rather follow someone on the force than that goofy, four-eyes any day. You've got my support if that happens." Grant finished off their conversation with the final nail in my coffin so to speak.

I could only sit and stare at the wall, their words cutting like a knife right through any courage that had been built up in me the night before in the sanitarium. I was considered a dud, a nobody. Well I was basically stuck there for the next few hours waiting for those two to leave, so I could save face. It was long after dark when I made my way back to my cabin. My mind was so involved in thinking about the events of the day that I did not see Ms. Peranio coming toward me. I was removed from my trance by a soft and gentle voice, "Good evening, Dr. Caldwell." I was taken aback. I had never spoken to her at the sanitarium. She probably knew of me though, seeing as we worked in the same building, I instantly felt butterflies in my stomach "He- hello, Ms. Peranio," I greeted her like a sophomore in high school.

"How are you on this first evening of our great adventure?"
"Is that what you would call all of this?" I replied.

"Well don't you think so too? Tell me, has anything in your life been as exciting as going after a lunatic turned killer? Not to mention, he obviously has ties to a very rich individual. There's just so much intrigue in this case, wouldn't you agree?" Again, I was aware of how nervous I was. "Almost too much intrigue if you ask me. You know the old saying, Ms. Peranio, 'curiosity killed the cat.'"

She looked confused and somewhat put out by my statement. I quickly tried to recover "What I meant was we are following a killer; catching up with Patronis is not going to be easy. There is a chance that some people may be hurt. I'm going to try to make sure that you are kept safe, Ms. Peranio, but I think you should reconsider how you are looking at this situation."

"I understand the risk, but I see the challenge as my glass half full, you see."
"I only wish I could live as carefree as you, Ms. Peranio."
Call me Mattie, please."
"If we are on a first name basis, you may call me Achiel."
"Achiel doesn't suit you very well, I like Ace instead. That is, if you don't mind."
"That's fine. Well goodnight, Ms. I mean Mattie." *When would I stop sounding so childish?*
Mattie just about purred, "Good night, Ace - pleasant dreams."

But I already knew that my dreams would be anything but pleasant.

Brighton Bay Sanitarium
Assistant Warden Achiel Caldwell's Log
April 16, 1949

(I was told by Dr. Ambridge to continue the use of Brighton Bay Sanitarium in my log seeing as someday when I am finished with my work, this log could be used by others within the sanitarium. Thus, even though my geographical position may change, the source and focus of my writing will remain constant.)

Today I woke up feeling a bit strange; I did not sleep very well again last night. The constant movement of the train felt odd to me. I went to the Diner Car and had a hard breakfast. It felt good to have some food in my stomach; I think it helped to steady my nerves a bit. I then went to the Game Room to try my hand at chess again. I was too late; the car was filled with people. There was only one seat open at a card table, so I sat down, not even noticing who sat across from me. "Hello" I heard the person say. Startled, I turned and saw the gigantic frame of Custos. He was dark-skinned and had large broad shoulders that made him look like a giant.

"How are we feeling today?" Custos was quite filled with himself.
"I can't complain," I replied.
"I don't think we were formally introduced. My name is Custos, I am Mr. Pista's personal bodyguard."

"Yes, my name is Dr. Caldwell, but you can call me Achiel if you wish. I've actually heard all about you from Dicere."

"Ahh... Yes, Dicere is a good messenger, but he tends to embellish things with his massive vocabulary."

"Forgive me for asking, but if you are Mr. Pista's personal bodyguard, then who is protecting him right now?"

"Mr. Pista has many protectors; currently he needs me to guide you and your team safely on your journey."

Now he had my attention. "Why? Are we in some sort of danger? I mean, we are just traveling to meet with Pista. We will not reveal anything to anyone about our plans after we meet with your boss."

"Achiel, there is always danger, no matter where you are. It lurks just outside your peripheral vision." It seemed to me that Custos enjoyed putting people in uncomfortable positions. "Danger bides its time watching you very closely; it is gauging when the optimal moment will present
itself. So never let your guard down; do not trust anyone. Focus your mind on the task at hand, and if you do so, no harm shall befall you."

I looked at him with questions plaguing me. But, he quickly turned the subject and asked if I would like to play an old card game he knew. He taught me how to play the game Karnoffel. We played for several hours, while we had an ongoing conversation. He told me all about Mr. Pista and how he was very wealthy and powerful. Before leaving he reached across the table to shake my hand. "It was very nice to have met you," he said. His hands felt like ice. He got up and began to walk away, I watched as a little girl ran from him to hide behind her mother, and a baby began to cry at the other end of the car. Custos did not appear to notice though, as he seemed to glide across the room. By the time we were finished, it was time for lunch. I returned to the Diner Car and got myself a hot dog, fries, and a drink. I went back to my room after lunch and realized my big meal had made me somewhat tired. I took a three-hour nap and was awakened by two people talking right outside my cabin. As I regained consciousness, I began to understand the direction of this conversation.

The Legends of Green Eagle
Interpreted by: Benito Cajero
Told by: Ta'awa Hotsko
Calabre II

Many days passed and the great man wandered the forests looking for animals. Finally, he became so tired that he sat down next to a large tree and leaned against it. He fell asleep, and when he awoke he found that there was something crawling on him. It was a poisonous spider. The man was so frightened he did not move. Then, all of a sudden, the spider was inhaled by a lizard that had been sitting on the tree. The man turned to look at the lizard, and that is when he knew this animal must be the first to be chosen. The man called out with a loud voice, "Quomvi Ta'aho, I wish that this animal might serve my needs." Then a voice came from the sky, "And so it shall be. You shall call these servants Soparli; they will serve as your army. When you are confronted with a foe, these soldiers will protect you. Use them well, oh good servant." And thus, the Soparli were given life and became a great army in the land.

I looked up from my book. It was too dark to read anymore, but overhead the stars and moon shown so brightly that they lit up the chairs and tables. I looked around and saw I was the only one left in the car. Or so I thought. Without warning a voice beckoned to me from the darkness in the corner of the rail car.

"What are you doing here?" My blood froze. I didn't want to answer, but I felt I had no choice. "Who are you?" I asked. "That is not important; what is important is that you go home." I had no idea who this was, but it sounded like a woman's voice. I thought it might be Mattie and Grant playing a trick on me. I became raging angry at the thought of those two snickering quietly in the shadows.

I answered, "I'm not going back and in time you will learn to respect my judgment and do as I say, because if you don't, I will send you home."

The voice was quiet for a moment. Then a low chuckle came from the corner where the mysterious voice originated. "I see that you want to become a leader. Silly human, I am telling you your mission is futile. You will never catch this man. He is too important to be captured by your kind."

I once again became unsure as to the source of the voice. "You obviously know things that you are not telling me," I said, still trying to be brave. There was silence again. "I am only here to warn you. You and your friends are being used. You are just brush strokes in a much larger painting than you could ever imagine. If you don't stop this foolish mission and return home, you and your friends will die." With that last word, the car door opened and the cigarette was extinguished. I ran as fast as I could to the door and looked out, feeling and seeing nothing. I turned the lights on in the Observatory Car, but still I did not find anything. It was as if I had been talking to a ghost.

I went back to my cabin more perplexed than when I had left. I tried again to get some sleep, troubled as it may be.

Brighton Bay Sanitarium
Assistant Warden Achiel Caldwell's Log
April 18, 1949

Yesterday was uneventful; Today, seemed to follow suit. I did notice that Grant looked much paler, as if he might be sick. He was very quiet as the group met in the Diner to discuss what would happen when we reached our destination later that day.

At about 7:00 p.m. the Streamliner arrived at a sleepy station in the small town of Kearny. It felt wonderful to walk on solid ground, even almost immediately after deboarding, the six of us got off of the train and were whisked away in two very nice, maroon Tucker Torpedoes. We must have gone over forty miles outside of the town when I began to see something in the distance shining brightly in the setting sun. As we got closer I could tell that this building was built almost entirely of glass. We pulled up to a ten-foot brick wall with a wrought-iron gate that had some sort of family crest on it. As soon as we drove through those gates the terrain changed drastically. Where outside the gate there was vast open space with nothing but sand in every direction; inside the gates there was a grand oasis. Palm trees loomed over our heads, and junipers sprouted everywhere. There were banana, peach, mango, pineapple, orange, and plum trees in a beautiful orchard. As we pulled up to the house, I could barely believe my eyes. The house seemed to be more like an observatory. On one side was an enormous greenhouse that must have stood twenty feet high; the other side looked like a Victorian-style castle with clear windows of various sizes facing in all four directions, allowing a massive amount of natural light in. The house also had plenty of odd statues sitting in certain areas, as if the house were being guarded by a silent stone army. Each statue looked a little different, but they all seemed to resemble animals. Their stone eyes seemed to glare at me as I got out of the car. Inside the greenhouse stood a grand Banyan tree that towered over us. Its roots reached almost to the front door, rendering us speechless. We walked inside and gawked at the amazing scenery. Tropical birds flew in every direction, and a beautifully clear pond that appeared almost like glass was located just to the south of the Banyan tree. Amid the wildlife stood a myriad of people who looked familiar, for they all wore the same clothing that Custos and Dicere wore. The only difference was that they all seemed to have different skin tones and ethnic origins.

On the east side of the entryway there was a large spiral staircase leading to upper rooms. The floors looked to be polished marble, and a brilliant, shining chandelier accented the space with a luminous glow. Dicere immediately left our party and ascended the staircase. We all stood in the foyer taking in its beauty. Upon closer examination, a sort of net-like partition kept all the wildlife from escaping the greenhouse area. I only found this out by walking straight into it. I heard a few muffled laughs behind me, but I didn't turn around; instead, I took in the breathtaking vegetation. There were small fruit trees in clusters around the edges of the pond. Bird of Paradise flowers grew up almost as sporadically as dandelions. I looked up and saw that there were also monkeys sitting on some of the branches of the Banyan tree.

Just then Dicere cleared his throat, and we all turned to see him standing at the top of the spiral staircase. "Mr. Pista welcomes you to his home, Natavis." Dicere's voice was almost robot-like. "He invites you to the dining room for refreshments. Then, when you finish, Ursa and Mendax shall show you to your rooms. Mr. Pista also says that tomorrow will be a day of rest and recovery from your travels. The following day he shall meet with you and discuss further plans."

With that, we went into the main dining room, which also had a glass skylight and partook of the finest fruits I had ever laid eyes on. There were pineapples twice the normal size, strawberries as big as my palm and oranges with a strange purple pulp. The colors of the fruit were vibrant, and their taste was so fresh and sweet that it almost gave me a sense I was dreaming. We then were led by Lupus to our rooms, which were located in a guest house directly behind the mansion. There were about eight single bedrooms in the place, along with a living quarters and a small kitchen and two washrooms. The journey so far had proved to be very exciting, but I found that yet again I had a hard time sleeping that night because of the excitement of wandering this fantasy land the next day.

Brighton Bay Sanitarium
Assistant Warden Achiel Caldwell's Log
April 19, 1949

I awoke early enough to see the sunrise this morning. The first majestic rays bounced off the glass dome of Natavis, making it glisten like a diamond. The grounds slowly started to take shape and degrees the beauty of the place took hold of me. I noticed that the mansion sat on an incline so that all of the land below could be clearly seen from the mansion windows. Small streams of water seemed to wind their way through the descending landscape. The water came from pumps that stood on either side of the mansion. The sun almost seemed to bring this oasis to life. I had not seen the extent of the grounds the night before, but as I looked this morning I saw that the palm trees and beautiful gardens stretched for several miles. The desert seemed to be kept out by the ten-foot solid brick wall that extended all the way around

61

the premises, similar to a moat surrounding a castle. I went out and began to walk the grounds. I saw a few laborers tending to the plants here and there; they seemed to me like monks and nuns working in their heavy, black cloaks with their hoods up. But mostly it seemed as though nature was doing its own work in this strange place. There were areas where the gravel path had all but disappeared under the foliage. It was as if no one could stop nature from working her wonders. I saw butterflies of colors I didn't know existed, more tropical birds of every type and occasionally a lime-colored lizard or two. The air was very warm, but it did not bother me because there was very low humidity; in fact, it was much better than the weather in Connecticut, where the cold of winter still clung to the sleeping trees and the dead plants at the sanitarium.

I must have spent all morning exploring the grounds, for at one o'clock a bell sounded from in the house and a loud voice that I figured to be Dicere's called out, "Lunch is served." I made my way back to the house and located the formal dining room. All of my companions had already gathered and were munching away on many of the same fruits that had been there the night before. Dicere raised his hands to quiet the room.

"Today we would like to invite our guests to go on a hunt with us for our supper. We will be hunting for a wild boar to bring to the table."

Benson practically wrung his hands together with anticipation and excitement. Custos raised his hands and let out a yell that sounded much like a native battle cry. He and a few other employees hurried from the room to make preparations. Grant still seemed to be very pale. He stood by the table with a blank expression on his face, staring off at the far wall. He almost seemed oblivious to the goings on in the room. I went over to Ms. Peranio and asked her about Grant's condition. She said he had told her he was not feeling well. I asked if she wouldn't mind taking him back to his room to rest. As I said this, Dicere came to my side.

"I noticed that your friend does not look so well. We have a medicine man here. His name is Artibus, and I can send him to attend to your friend if you wish." It was the first time anyone had asked for my permission. It seemed strange, but this magical place had made me forget that I was supposed to oversee this trip. I told Dicere to send this man Artibus to check on Grant.

A man in a cloak grabbed my arm before I could leave the room. He thrust a bow and a quiver of arrows into my hands and said, "Today, little man, you become a hunter." I couldn't help but smile at him. He then proceeded to practically drag me out of the house and down to the gardens, where the rest of the hunting party waited. Custos set us up in a line, putting a man about every twenty feet. We made somewhat of a human wall. He then took out two of his arrows and began to smack them together. We all copied him as we entered the overgrown forest.

I had walked for about a mile when I heard a loud rustle to my left and then in a second a large boar crashed through the undergrowth. Unfortunately for me the boar was not retreating like I thought it would. Instead it turned its black bulging eyes upon me and began to charge. I let out a yell for help as I clumsily grabbed at an arrow and fit it into my bow. It was then I realized I hadn't shot a bow and arrow since my grade school years. I was in a very bad spot, but I notched the arrow and pulled it back as far as I could, but as I did my fingers slipped and the arrow went whizzing off. It ricocheted off the boar's back and struck home in a tree over to the right. By now the boar was only ten feet from me, barreling at top speed. I dropped the bow and readied myself to leap out of the way. I did so and just in time, as the boar caught my foot with his tusk as he passed. My leap suddenly turned into an awkward flip, and I landed hard on my back. Even though I felt all the air punched out of my lungs, I instinctively sat up to look where the boar was. I was surprised to find he had fallen, and simultaneously I noticed the arrow sticking out of its back. I lay back down and tried to catch my breath. I saw Custos running out from behind some trees with a huge knife. He made quick work of what life the boar may have had left and then ran over to me to check on me. I gave him the thumbs up sign and he must have known that meant I was fine. He looked at my foot where the boar had struck me. "How does your foot feel?" He asked. I gingerly moved my foot first and everything seemed fine, but I screamed in pain when I attempted to move my toes. Custos grabbed at my shoe and gently slid it off my foot. "Don't look," he said to me as he gently removed the sock. By this time Benson and the other two had approached. I could tell by looking at Benson's face that something was terribly wrong. Then I felt a tug and heard a snapping sound. I grabbed at the ground with both hands and screamed. I must have passed out right there, because when I awoke, I was being carried back on a crudely constructed stretcher. I looked up at Benson. "You all right, Dr. Caldwell?" I shook my head and looked around. The two servants were carrying me back to the house and two more were carrying the boar, which was hog-tied to a large stick and was swinging back and forth. Custos came to my side, "I am very sorry, Dr. Caldwell, I did not know you were not an experienced hunter." Mr. Benson scoffed. "You can tell that from just looking at him? No offense, Doc?" Custos looked ashamed and then he bent down closer to me. "I know who you are; I got the message. I have been watching you for some time. I had an inkling you might be him." Benson spoke up again, "At least you hit something, Dr. Caldwell. You happened to peg an iguana to that tree you hit. It caused quite a stir among the other men in our party." He almost sounded proud. I looked up at Custos, who seemed to be furrowing his brow into a snarl. The two workers carrying my stretcher both looked angry as well.

When we got back to Natavis I was carried into the room where Grant was reclining. They put me in a bed next to him, and Custos said he would send Artibus to take a look at my toe. With that they all left the room and it fell quiet. I looked over at Grant. He still laid rigid, staring straight at the ceiling. Then I noticed there were ropes coming up the sides of the bed. I looked closer: he was tied to the bed! It startled me. Why would they tie him there? It made no sense.

"Grant, can you hear me? What happened to you? Why do they have you tied down?" I looked inquisitively at him. His head slowly turned and his eyes focused on me. His face was whiter than the sheets that lay sandwiched between him and the bed.

"Help me," he said under his breath.

"Help me!" he whispered again and began to struggle mightily, trying in vain to free himself. I got up out of my bed and gingerly hobbled over to him. I attempted to free his bonds, but as I did a voice shouted at me from the doorway, "Do not release him." It was Artibus. He came in with four orderlies. "Remove him from this room." Artibus ordered coldly. I felt the tight grip of strong hands as one of the men began to pull me from the room. I watched in horror as Grant struggled mightily on the bed, "Cover his mouth so he doesn't scream," Artibus directed and one of the workers did so. I tried my hardest to struggle against the strong hands that were dragging me. As I was being pulled out the door I managed to grab hold of the frame with both hands. I hung on for all I was worth, watching as the doctor and his three assistants crowded around Grant. I heard his muffled screams. "Hold him still! I have to get it out," I heard Artibus say. Then a searing pain hit me like a bag of bricks right in the front of my brain. I instinctively let go of the door frame and crumpled onto the floor. My ears instantly began to ring and I felt paralyzed. I must have passed out, because when I came to I was back in the bed across from Grant. Artibus was applying a salve to my toe, which was a hideous blackish-blue color right around the joint.

"Glad you have finally come to," Artibus remarked.

"I am applying a mixture of Eucalyptus nectar and ground cocoa bean. The eucalyptus is to take the swelling down and the cocoa is to stimulate healing. I've also brought you a splint to keep your toe from moving too much. You should probably stay in bed the rest of the day."

I noticed Grant turn over in his bed, letting out a moan as he did so. Then my memory flashed and I looked at Artibus. He must have known the question was coming. He looked at me and said, "Your friend is going to be fine." I looked over again and saw he was not bound to the bed as he had been and did not look as pale anymore; in fact, he looked like he was almost back to his normal olive pigment now.

"What happened to him? Why did you have him tied down?" Artibus looked at me inquisitively,

"Tied down?" he questioned. Mr. Grant had a fever this afternoon; it seemed to be coming from a parasite that was inside his body. All I had to do was flush it out of his system."

He held up a jar of what looked like honey. "Have you ever seen Amber, Dr. Caldwell?" I nodded my head yes.

"Well this is Agave Nectar. Once it enters the body it acts as a net, catching anything that might be living on the inside and wrapping it so tightly that it smothers it. It then passes the culprit out of the body. That's what we did to your friend here."

I looked at him closely, trying to see if there were any signs that he could be lying. I saw nothing. Did I imagine all that happened just minutes before? I was unsure. Artibus left the room rather quickly after our conversation, and I was left alone with my thoughts. It wasn't long before I could not take it anymore, and I limped to my room and grabbed my green leather book and began to read.

The Legends of Green Eagle
Interpreted by: Benito Cajero
Told by: Ta'awa Hotsko
Calabre III

The Great Man spent many moons teaching his new servants how to accomplish certain tasks, He taught them about the sun and how it caused the plants to grow. He showed them the arts of growing and harvesting fruit. Then he tried to teach them how to build. But try as he might, these Soparli could not build things. So the Great Man left his new servants and spent many days brooding in a cave. One morning as he was sleeping he heard the ground quaking underneath him. As he watched, a mole stuck its head up through the dirt. The man instantly knew he had found his builder. "Quomvi Ta'aho, I wish to have a new animal serve me. I want the moles to be my builders." A voice bellowed, "Great Man, you shall have your wish. This animal shall build you palaces above and below the earth. You shall call them 'Sapator'. These new creatures shall also find you great wealth that is hidden from sight. May they serve you well." And with that the Great Man had a new servant to teach.

It was dusk when my door opened and in came Ms. Peranio.

"Achiel, how are you? Are you in much pain?"
"Not as long as I don't move. I feel fine."

69

Chuckling, Mattie replied, "Well I brought you a bit of dinner, seeing as you helped drop it.

"Mattie that was kind of you! What do you think of this place?" I must admit, I was tickled to have Mattie to myself, even if it was only for a few moments.

"I'm blown away. It is awe inspiring, majestic almost. But," and here her voice seemed to become thicker, lower. "There seems to be an undertone of fear. I can't seem to get it out of the back of my mind. It's like someone is whispering 'beware' in my ear."

"Now that you mention it, I think I've gotten that sense too. Like my mind is telling me this is all too good to be true."

"Exactly! I went to see Grant just before I came to see you. It's like he can't hear me He looks like he's asleep; tossing and turning and mumbling things under his breath but he will not wake up. I even tried to shake him awake, but he never opened his eyes. Did Artibus say what he thought was wrong with him?"

As a nurse, it was clear she was trying to reason this out. "He said Grant had a parasite that gave him a raging fever."

"What parasite? When could he have ingested a parasite? You don't think he picked it up on the train, do you?"

"I don't know, but he did not look pale before yesterday," I replied.

"Oh, I almost forgot. Custos gave me this walking stick for you. Just in case you needed to use the restroom or something. Well, I better get going I need to get some sleep before the big powwow tomorrow."

I thanked her again for bringing the dinner and the cane and she left.

I had forgotten that tomorrow would be the day we planned a strategy to find Patronis. It had been an odd day, and now the moon shown through the small window in my room. I picked up the walking stick and used it to hobble to the door of the guest house. I wanted to see the mansion again, with its greenhouse all lit up from the chandelier. It was even more gorgeous at night than it was in the day. I took a step outside the door and immediately froze. It was as if someone had flipped a switch. Soft lights began to come on all over the grounds. The lights seemed to be turning on in a circuit. Light came on close to the mansion first and then more and more of them ignited in the direction of the back wall, until the whole place was lit with a soft glow. It was then I saw Custos. He was standing only about ten feet in front of me, but he did not look at me. Instead he scanned the dark night sky, "You should not be out here this night Achiel." He spoke as if in a trance and without looking at me. "Is something wrong?" I asked him. He then stopped scanning the sky and gave me a concerned look, "Are you all right? How is your toe?" he asked, seeming to change the subject.

"I'm fine, Custos. What is going on here? It seems as if everyone is hiding things, and I'm confused by all of this." I didn't really care what I said anymore; there were just too many weird things happening for me not to reveal what everyone from our party was thinking. Custos looked down at the ground and then back at me "You will understand better after tomorrow. Now please go up to your room. You need rest." I agreed, but as I turned I glimpsed about four other servants spread out over the grounds, and they all had their heads thrown back and were looking at the sky. I now knew something very strange was going on. I went back to my room, thinking the entire way. In spite of my conviction that extraordinary things were happening, I slept soundly for the first time in about a week.

Brighton Bay Sanitarium
Assistant Warden Achiel Caldwell's Log
April 20, 1949

When I woke up this morning, the sun was already high in the sky. I must have slept very hard, because there was a pool of wet saliva on my pillow. I quickly shook off the cobwebs and got dressed. I put my green leather-bound book in my waist-coat pocket. My toe hurt even worse today, so I did not attempt to put a shoe on my left foot but rather left it bare. I picked up the walking stick that Custos gave me and limped up to the main house. Everyone else had already gathered in the main dining area for breakfast. Most of the employees were in the room as well. I saw that even Grant was up and around, looking somewhat back to his normal self. The only person missing from our party was Dicere. I quickly grabbed a couple pieces of fruit to munch on, while a few of the servants approached me to ask about how my foot was doing. Artibus came over and took a look as well; he seemed to think the salve was doing the trick. After about twenty minutes of pleasantries, one of the servants called us out to the foyer. We all emerged, and there was Dicere standing at the top of the stairs. "It is time," he announced. His voice was rather loud yet very articulate.

Dr. Caldwell, Mr. Pista will see you now." I froze and glanced at my other friends. Ms. Peranio, Benson and Grant all turned their puzzled faces to me. I walked to the top of the stairs slowly, where Dicere still waited for me.

"Dicere, I thought this whole planning thing was going to be a joint effort by the group." As I said this I pointed to the rest of my party waiting downstairs.

"Mr. Pista has always wanted to meet and talk with you, Doctor; he knows you have inside knowledge on Patronis. Dr. Ambridge told him all about how you were in direct contact with him." I couldn't deny that Dicere tried to dispel the situation. "Mr. Pista will confer with Dr. Caldwell first and then Dr. Caldwell will bring the plan that they propose to the rest of us."

I looked down at Benson, who was starting to flush a bright red color in his cheeks. He spoke, "So let me get this straight. Dr. Caldwell gets to see Mr. Pista, and we must follow whatever plan Mr. Pista and the doctor decide to formulate, even if we take issue with it?" Dicere never took his eyes off Benson the entire time he was speaking.

"Yes, that was always the plan. Achiel was deemed the leader of the group by Dr. Ambridge. You will do as you are told; otherwise, I believe there is a train headed back east leaving tomorrow that Mr. Pista would be willing to put you on." Benson's wild look began to settle, even though there were still undertones of quiet rage discernible in him. Dicere continued, "Anyone else?" he asked somewhat dramatically. There was no answer, so he turned to me and said, "Let me show you to Mr. Pista's room."

He led me down a corridor and at the end of it stood two large men, who were obviously guarding the intricately designed, double doors that led into Mr. Pista's room. They stood aside, opened the doors and a flood of light came spilling out onto the dense Berber carpet in the hall. Dicere entered first and announced my presence. I walked in slowly. The room had nothing in it but a large four poster bed with see-through curtains that hung down to the floor on every side. The walls on the east and west were covered with paintings of what looked like warring beasts and other fascinating but unrecognizable characters. I made my way over to the bed and saw there was a chair positioned beside it. I sat down before looking at Mr. Pista. There was the man who was responsible for all of the beauty I had witnessed in Natavis. He was old, wrinkled and bald, but his eyes still looked full of life. They were that same emerald green as all the other Natavis employees. When he spoke, his voice was soft and airy.

"Hello there, Doctor Caldwell, my name is Draxman Pista. I am very glad you have chosen to go on this mission for me. I would love to accompany you, but alas, I am too old and am not able to even leave my bed anymore."

I was awed but found my voice. "It's nice to finally meet you, sir. My companions and I have all loved our stay here at Natavis; it is an exquisite place."

I'm glad you have found it to your liking." He was brisk and business-like. "I'm sure you are wondering why we are out here in the middle of nowhere. Well, Doctor I have been conducting many experiments here in the desert in order to help food production for the United States government. We work mostly with fruits and vegetables trying to get them to grow bigger and produce more fruit. In fact, Mr. Patronis was one of my top scientists his discoveries have been revolutionary. Now you see why I must get him back."

I shook my head to show that I understood "What about the clothes you all wear? Why the black robes?"

Pista smiled "I'm sure we look somewhat strange to you, but you see, we are all naturalists. Our garments are a sign of our diligence to this religion. We all worship nature and help to nourish it as well. Our garments are made out of and dyed by the plants we produce here at Natavis."

With that Pista changed the subject, "If you don't mind, I would like to get down to it. Can you tell me of your interactions with Mr. Gabriel Patronis?"

I took quite a while explaining what had happened back in Brighton: how Patronis had eluded our facility and yet how he had left many clues behind. Mr. Pista finally cut in: "It seems as if Mr. Patronis was leaving a trail for someone to follow him. Did you jot down any of these markings or writings he left in his room?"

I was impressed with his observations. "Why yes, I scribbled them in this book."

The Legends of Green Eagle's Fables -_how did you happen to come by such a book?"

"My grandmother gave it to me. She used to read it to me when I was a boy."

It was obvious that Pista was more than familiar with it. "The stories told within these pages tell tales of a history forgotten. Ahh, here are the drawings, Hmm...... I see he was making a key with his drawings. Here look... see the 'X' there in the heart of Mexico? I believe he is headed there to find an ancient relic."

"What? You mean that these scribbles of a crazy man actually lead to where he was going?" It was becoming more obvious to me.

"Yes, Dr. Caldwell, sometimes, if a person is not understood by the public, the easiest way to dispose of them is to hide them behind walls. In Mr. Patronis's case, those walls were the sanitarium. In the modern era, you are considered a grown-up when you leave childish tendencies behind. One of those tendencies is believing in fantasy. Believing that the world consists of more than the eye can see. Mr. Patronis believes there are things on this earth that go unseen by the human eye. Does that make him crazy, Dr. Caldwell? Now that does not mean that Gabriel is somehow safe; he is still very dangerous and should be treated as such."

"That depends," I slowly responded. I knew I had to think carefully before speaking.

"Depends? Depends on what, exactly?"
"Well, on whether there are things that go unseen."

"Ahh, but who can make that call?" Pista arrogantly asked. "Who is checking to see whether Mr. Patronis is right? You see, Doctor, it is a vicious circle and ultimately those stuck on the outside are the people deemed 'insane' or in other societies 'outcasts'." We were now speaking my language. "Yes, but I believe that we can tell if a person is psychologically insane from a young age. They do not need to be considered an adult to have psychological issues."

"Perhaps, Doctor, there may be some cases where you can detect certain signs, but for the most part, those are the rarities. When was the last time you locked up a child for fearing that a monster lived under his bed?"
"I see. You think it is a societal norm for a child to have an imagination and believe in monsters."

"Somewhat true, but what if I told you that imagination had nothing to do with it."

"You mean to say these children really do see monsters under their beds?" I was somewhat confused.

"Would it be so hard to open your mind, Doctor, to the existence of so-called 'monsters'? Or would that make you 'insane'? You see, there are those special people who cannot shake the 'monsters' in their lives. Patronis is one of those. Remember that as you go searching for him. Enough of Psychology. I must tell you of the relic he seeks. It is well known. Perhaps you have heard of the 'Fountain of Youth'?"

Now I was stunned. "Of course, everyone has heard of that story. The water is supposed to prolong life – right?"

"Exactly! A person could have everlasting life if he possessed the fountain."

I tried to remember my Spanish history. "But wasn't it supposed to be a waterfall somewhere? And by possess, don't you mean occupy the area where it is geographically located?"

"In some tales it is thought to be a waterfall, but in others it is just a small boulder with the center carved out. The water magically comes out of the rock and pools in the indentation.

"Almost like the Bible story, when Moses struck the rock in the desert and water came...."

"No need to bring the Bible into this; many religions have a story about mystical events. Pista retorted without letting me finish. "It's the same concept, but this one is continuous; it never stops flowing. Anyway, I believe the story that Patronis is following originates in your book here. Quomvi Ta'aho', so the story goes, created a gift for 'the Great Man Dominebris'. The gift was supposed to keep him and his servants alive for eternity. It is said in the book that this 'Man' hid the gift in order to keep it safe. The book also hints that the 'Man' and his descendants lived in the south."

Still thinking out loud, I postulated, *"Green Eagle* lived in New Mexico, right? So that would make south somewhere in either Central or South America. But how did Patronis know to pick Mexico?"

"It is said that before Benito Cajero died, someone approached him to ask about old *'Green Eagle'*. The only thing that Cajero could say about him is that supposedly he was the ancestor of a long all-but-extinct tribe from the south, whose cities still exist as a reminder of the tribe's former greatness.

"The Mayans? Yes, it makes sense that they originated in Mexico."

"Some believe that the Mayans built their cities to mirror the stars," Pista pointed out. "I believe our best bet is to find the city that sits under the Ursa Minor. This past week I have been looking for ancient ruins that sit under this constellation. I first sent a man down to Mexico to ask around for an archeologist who might know of an ancient Mayan city like that."

"Excuse me, Mr. Pista, but you said you have been doing all this for the past week? We just got here two days ago. Are you telling me you knew where he was headed and you didn't send any of your own men after him?"

"Hmmm…about Patronis: I had no physical proof about where he was headed until I saw your drawings here today. Now where was I? Oh yes, take a look at this map. That 'X' there is the location of the ancient Mayan city 'Kul'; it is the exact astronomical position of the star Polaris. I tend to believe you will find Patronis heading for this temple."

"But that temple is in the midst of the Yucatan Peninsula! Isn't that area covered in dense jungles?" I wanted to know.

"The jungle is the least of your worries. There will be unfriendly natives, biting insects, and poisonous serpents and plants. This journey will be very dangerous. That is why I am sending a group of my men with you to keep you safe as best they can."

"Do you think you could send Custos with us as well? I'm beginning to enjoy his companionship." I didn't want to sound like I was begging. "I know he is your personal bodyguard, but I would feel better about this arduous journey if you could send him with us."

"Well, if you wish you may have him. I must inform you he was to be punished for his mishandling of the situation yesterday. He almost got you killed. You are lucky to still be alive."

I looked at things differently. "Yes, well if it weren't for his arrow, I would be dead right now; he killed the boar before it could attack me a second time. I owe my life to that man."

"That is something that we share, a common bond so to speak. You may take Custos, but I will be keeping Dicere here. I need him to help convey my requests to the other staff."

"All right, it's a deal. Now, for the rest of your plan."

"Ah, yes, you shall take Custos, Procul, Mendax, Fortis and Omnus with you on your journey. I have arranged for a flight that leaves two days from now. You will land in Tulum, where Manus, my servant, is waiting for you. He has assembled a team to travel into the jungle with you. He says he has an archeologist, an explorer, a doctor and a group of natives who will travel with you. He says the explorer thinks it will take approximately two weeks to reach the site - if it is out there. The archeologist adds that this site has never been found or excavated before, so it may be hard to come across it. His plans are for all of you to go see Muyil, another Mayan city, to get an idea of what you are looking for. From there, you will hike southwest into the jungle some forty miles from Muyil.

Along with this information, Manus also sent a list of supplies you should bring. I took the liberty of buying them and putting them in camping bags. Dicere will go over all of that with you tomorrow."

I was furiously trying to absorb all this, jotting down what I could. "Forgive me if I seem a bit skeptical, but this trip and everything has happened so quickly; I feel like I'm in some sort of weird nightmare."

Pista saw my confusion. "Do you think it a mere accident that you were chosen to lead this delegation? Ah, Dr. Caldwell, you were carefully investigated. You were selected because you are indeed the perfect man for the job."

"It is a lot to take in," Pista nodded as he spoke. "But I must reinforce how delicate the work is that we are doing here. I must stress that you are to confide in no one the information I have shared with you here. In addition, I have a bit of advice for you, Doctor. Don't be afraid to open your eyes on this journey, even though the social norms and your companions may look down upon that. Even if you have to rationalize that you are doing so just to get a glimpse of what Patronis sees, it might end up saving your life. Speaking of sight, I was wondering if you wouldn't mind if I take a look at those eyes of yours. Yes, come closer, Doctor; I am old and short of sight.

I leaned in close, and he took off my spectacles to peer into my eyes.

Leaning back, Pista reached over toward a side table and said, "I am willing to give you a reward for all of your work so far in this case, Doctor. Are you willing to receive it?"

There was a plant on the table, and he dug inside the pot and grabbed at something and held it out to me.

Mystified, I asked, "What is that?"

"It is just the root of a plant. You need to eat it."

Warily, I took the root and gingerly placed it in my mouth and began to chew. There was an earthy taste, but it was followed by a sweet yet spicy taste that reminded me of black licorice mixed with bourbon. I suddenly felt tingly all over. In a split second I was frozen. My body seemed transfixed to that spot. I could not even blink. Mr. Pista had squeezed a leaf on the plant and there was juice on his fingers. He rubbed the juice between his thumbs and then, before I could say anything or even mumble, he stuck his thumbs right into my eyes! I wanted to scream from the pain. It was as if someone was taking little needles and mixing my corneas. There was a bright white flash that flew past my vision and then nothing but darkness for a few seconds. Slowly I began to see stars, and light began to filter back into my eyes. Dim outlines seemed to appear next. All the while the searing pain began to decrease. After a few minutes, I could see clearly again, but my eyes had a dimension I had never experienced. They began to focus in on color and shape contrasts. Then I noticed a slight movement on the plant on the other side of the bed, and my eyes focused even further. It was a gnat sitting on one of the leaves, but I could see it very clearly. I had never had vision like this before; in fact, my eyesight had been quite bad since I was young.

"I think that will do it," Pista announced. "Here now, I gave you a very powerful sedative. I want you to focus all your energy on swallowing. This is a fermented herbal tea that will rid your system of the sedative."

He gave me a drink, and slowly sensation began returning to my limbs. I gasped for breath as if I had been under water the entire time. As soon as I could speak I demanded of him, "What did you just do to me?"

"Take a look around, Doctor," Pista was almost lecturing me. "I have cleared your vision, but the vision you seek does not come from your eyes. For there is more to the world than meets the eye. I think that will conclude our meeting. Dicere, Doctor Caldwell is ready to reveal our plan to the others."

With that Dicere entered the room again and motioned for me to leave. As I was exiting I heard. Pista say, "If you don't mind, I think I will keep your spectacles as a memento to the old you."

I worked hard trying to wrap my mind around what just happened. I was, after all, a learned man. There was simply no explanation and that frustrated me. I realized suddenly that these past twenty-four hours had been nothing but frustrating.

It was lunch time when I was sent back down the stairs. I found Benson, Grant and Ms. Peranio gathered around the dining room table. They all looked at me inquisitively, partly because they didn't know why Pista had just talked to me, and partly because I did not have my glasses anymore. I told them to come down to the guest house so we could talk. They all followed me down so as to avoid a public confrontation. It was there that I explained to them my entire ordeal with Pista. I talked about where we were being sent, how he thought Patronis was not crazy, and how he had healed my eyes. When I finished recounting my experiences, they all just stood there, stunned into silence. Grant was the first to speak.

"It sounds a lot like what that crazy doctor of theirs did to me. He put this root down my throat and I couldn't even think. Then he followed with some sort of liquid, and even though I couldn't feel anything and could only stare at the ceiling, I could hear my body writhing under me. It was other worldly, but when it was over I felt like I had returned to normal."

"You never told us what ailed you, Grant," Ms. Peranio asked.

"Oh, I wasn't sick; it was just that I was losing control of my body. It started in my extremities. My legs started moving without me realizing it but it wasn't spastic movement. Rather, my legs began to walk without me knowing that I wanted to walk; my arms would reach and grab things and I could not even feel them do so. Then my mouth succumbed. I couldn't call out for help. It was as if my spirit was trapped inside a mechanical being that acted completely on its own."

"That couldn't have been," Ms. Peranio exclaimed. "No parasite in the known world could take over your body and make you move in cognitive ways; it's impossible. I saw you looking around in the greenhouse the other day. It takes a lot of coordination not to trip on any of those roots that come from the Banyan Tree."

Grant stared off into space as he answered. "It wasn't a parasite. It was as if something or someone else was moving and talking for me."

"That's impossible!" Ms. Peranio was clearly not buying his explanation. "Why would something or someone want to take over your body, Grant?"

I offered my opinion. "I'm beginning to think we cannot rule anything out."

"Doc, you should call Ambridge. Tell him how crazy this all is. He can get us back. We don't have to go through with this."

"I agree. I don't like this anymore; something is very wrong with this whole situation." Mattie was more emotional than I had ever seen her.

"It's too late for that. Ambridge told me before I left that if I didn't come home with Patronis, I was not to come home at all. His job is on the line in this situation. I must continue. But you three are free to head back to Brighton. I would not blame you for doing so."

There was silence for a few moments and then Ms. Peranio spoke up.

"Knowing I did not see this journey through to completion, I would feel guilty for the rest of my   life. I'm with you, Doctor Caldwell."
Grant was the next to speak, "If Ambridge loses his job, more than likely I lose mine too. I will stay as well."

Finally, Benson commented, "Might I just say, you all should get locked up in that sanitarium after this adventure. I'll come along too."
"I know it seems as if this journey was foolish from the get-go. I also know that all three of you did not agree with the thought of me leading this mission. Well from now on, we will make decisions as a team.   I promise you."

"I like the sound of that," Benson declared.
"Me too," Grant chimed in.

"All right, green eyes! What do we do now?" Mattie had a tease to her voice

"To whom are you talking?" I asked.

"Why, you of course," Mattie replied. "I guess I never saw the true color of your eyes under those huge glasses you always wore."

"My eyes are blue, so I don't know what you're talking about."

Grant insisted, "Well, they are green now. In fact, they look almost the same color as all the people around here. Do you think when he did that thing to your eyes he changed...."

But I wasn't listening any longer. I was running for the mirror. I looked and there they were, plain as day: emerald-green eyes! I was taken aback. What had Pista done to me?

Before I went to bed that night Artibus lightly knocked on my door. I let him in, and he made me lie down on the bed while he examined my toe again. I asked him, "What happened to Grant that made him do what he did? I mean, he was fully functional and yet he seemed so far off No parasite I know of can cause that type of sickness."

Artibus brought out his salve and applied it again to the area, rubbing very vigorously above the toe and on the underside as well. It hurt like the dickens, but I knew that the salve was supposed to help, so I grit my teeth and hoped his incessant rubbing would stop soon. After he finished he answered me, "Sometimes there are types of diseases that creep into the body undetected. These diseases cannot be cured with potions or medicines of any kind. Instead they must be pulled from the body like pulling a tooth. That is what happened to your friend. He simply needed his tooth pulled, so to speak." Artibus smiled and then asked, "By the way, have you seen Grant lately? I knocked on his door but he did not answer." I shrugged my shoulders, for I had no idea where he was. With that Artibus turned and left. My foot felt very sore after that, so I took out my little green leather-bound book and began to read.

The Legends of Green Eagle
Interpreted by: Benito Cajero
Told by: Ta'awa Hotsko
Calabre IV

After the Great Man had helped the Sapator to build many great cities, he began to feel his age. By this time the Great Man was very old indeed. He caught a sickness and wearily made his way southeast until he came to a bay with beautiful white sand and glassy, turquoise waters. It was there he saw a school of fish jump from the water. "Quomvi Ta'aho hear me now, for I am old and am dying. Grant me this one last kindness. Let the fish of that school serve me." A voice answered through the waves of the ocean. "Oh, Great Man, I shall grant you this. The fish you have chosen shall serve you, and you shall call them Syreni. They shall keep great treasures in the deep dark places. They will also deliver unto you messages from abroad. They will serve you in places where no man can go. As he was speaking a beautiful woman appeared from out of the water. She was carrying what looked like a stone clutched to her breast. She came closer to land. As she came towards the Great Man, he could see that her upper half was human, but her lower half consisted of scales and fins. "Behold," said Quomvi Ta'aho, "She brings you a gift from the secret places below the tide." With that the man walked out to her and took the rock that was filled with clear water. "Taste of this water every day, you and your servants, and you shall live forever." The

Great Man did as he was told and instantly his illness subsided and he went away cured from his ailments.

Brighton Bay Sanitarium
Assistant Warden Achiel Caldwell's Log
April 21, 1949

The following morning I awoke late again. I felt very rested, and my toe felt much better as well. I was greeted at breakfast by Custos, who noticed I had less of a limp today. He promised to show me something very interesting later on.

After breakfast Dicere gathered the group of us going to Mexico and showed us the gear we would be taking. There were shirts and trousers made of a certain material that was supposed to stand up well against the harsh and wet conditions of the rain forest. Moisture-reducing socks that would keep our feet dry so we would not get trench foot were also included. We were given flexible climbing boots that would help us against the terrain. Finally, we were each issued a camping bag that contained two extra pairs of shirts and trousers, four changes of socks. also included were eighteen dehydrated meals (mostly fruits), a knife, a 20-foot rope, fishing line and hooks, a mosquito net, a hanging hammock, a half-liter canteen, a compass, a flare gun with a box of ten flares, a machete, binoculars and a Tilley Hat. Needless to say all that gear made the packs somewhat heavy, but Dicere insisted each item was necessary, so we just nodded and agreed. He then went through a brief summary of certain plants we might see that may prove helpful if we had an injury or needed food. I wasn't really paying attention; my mind was churning over what Pista had said the day prior. "There is more to this world than meets the eye." I tried to imagine what Patronis saw in the world. Did he really see monsters? Later that day Custos took me up to the mansion to where one of the pumps propelled water out onto the ground. Next to the pump was a metal grate that he removed, and he climbed down a ladder inside. I followed him, and deep inside was a long shaft with a large pipe. It seems I was looking at the life source for Natavis. Two three hundred-foot wells were dug deep into the sand in the upper corners of the property. The water was then sucked up the pipes and fed down the property in winding streams. Once it reached the bottom of the hill, it was drained into twelve-foot wells, which in turn fed underground aqueducts that went slowly downward and fed an underwater lake. He showed me a set of stairs leading down. Sure enough, at the bottom of the stairs was a large lake. The water was then fed into pipes that descended to the base of the original three hundred-foot wells. The lake seemed to be encircled by a cave. Custos told me that when Pista found the place, it was nothing more than a hill of sand covering an empty cave. He then told me to turn, and as I did I saw three four-foot holes in the north cave wall. They were letting sunlight stream into the water. Where the light hit the water, you could see straight to the bottom, which was so unusual, because it had to be more than twenty feet deep in the middle. Custos said the holes were capped with three different magnifying glasses, which focused the light on the water warming the underground lake enough to support fish such as Tilapia. It was beautiful to take in.

Custos went on to say that this water source was only the first half of the magic that made Natavis the oasis it was. The large man explained how Pista had a bulldozer come in and put a slight descending grade to the area. Then he had truck load upon truck load of coconut rind and wood chips brought out into the middle of the desert; enough to have a layer about a foot deep spread across the twenty-acre sloping property. A thin layer of fertilizer was spread below the wood chips. Then Pista planted all the fruit and tropical forestry that has since ravenously taken over Natavis's clean slate. As soon as a year later, Pista started to introduce tropical creatures to the landscape. Their excrement kept up the fertilizer supply on the surface of Natavis. Thus, the tropical oasis was born. The only plant that was not started from seed was the Banyan Tree, which was brought from Mexico by way of semi.

That evening I took myself down into the cave to look at the pond. The sun was starting to set, sending orange light through the lake. I could see the schools of tilapia swimming through the sun spots. I felt the calm water with my hand; it was quite warm. The sun's rays did an excellent job of heating the lake, which otherwise would be quite cold. The place was quiet and serene. The only sound was the slight whoosh of the pumps from the wells above and the trickle of water as it fed back into the lake. It was a good place to reflect on the events of this week. Pista's words were still very unsettling to me; I could not understand what he meant when he told me to "Open my mind." I was confused. Who were these people here at Natavis? There were many things about them that were strange. The laborers seemed to behave as though Pista was their king, and Pista had healed my eyes. Something was very different about all of this. It was as though I had suddenly stepped into a different world that most people would never have the chance to see in their lifetime.

I walked back to the guest house as twilight put the whole landscape to sleep. Once again the lights began to turn on and extend outward down the slope of Natavis. I walked past Custos, who had assumed the same position he had been in the night prior. His eyes were transfixed on the sky. "Goodnight, Achiel," he said without taking his gaze away from the starlit sky. "Good night, Custos," I responded as I walked through the door and up into my room. I wanted to read more of my book. It seemed to clear my mind and help me to sleep better.

The Legends of Green Eagle

Interpreted by: Benito Cajero
Told by: Ta'awa Hotsko
Calabre V

For a time, the Great Man and his servants built a beautiful kingdom filled with cities and gardens that extended many miles through the forest. The Great Man became lonely. He had his servants, but Quomvi Ta'aho had promised him "people" to go along with his servants. So, he cried out, "Quomvi Ta'aho, you have promised me many things and you have been faithful to deliver those gifts to me, but you promised me people, so that I may establish my kingdom. A voice called out of the storm clouds, like deep rumbling thunder "I have given you all that you need. Yet, you ask for more I am no servant that answers to your every whim. If you want me to do this for you, you must first perform an act of service for me. There are people to the north; they live in huts and villages that pale in comparison to the cities you and your servants have built. If you want people willing to inhabit your lands, you must burn their villages and kill those who resist you. Then when they have submitted to you and your power, you must collect ten of their children and burn them as a sacrifice to me." The Great Man was struck with horror. He did not want to hurt anyone, especially children. Quomvi Ta'aho continued, "You and your servants shall rule over the kingdom of mankind forever; you shall control them with your mighty hand." The Great Man went deep into the forest to be alone and to think about what Quomvi Ta'aho had told him.

Brighton Bay Sanitarium
Assistant Warden Achiel Caldwell's Log
April 22, 1949

Today was our last day in Natavis. I was somewhat sad to be leaving this place of unbelievable beauty. The fear of finding and facing Patronis had also returned. The day was spent relaxing and preparing for the trip the following day. Artibus found me and gave me a small vile of the salve he had been rubbing on my toe. Custos, Procul, and Mendax were all loading a large army truck with our backpacks and supplies. I walked the property again, setting a slow pace. I took a closer look at every tree, bush and plant. The colors seemed to be so much more vivid since Pista enhanced my eyesight. Towards evening, Dicere called us all into the house and shared the plans for tomorrow. We were to load the army truck at seven o'clock sharp and drive to an airfield that was only a few miles away. There we would be loaded into a Douglas C-47 Sky train that would fly us to Tulum, a small city where the rest of our party would be waiting for us. I felt the need to go to bed early, but I could not fall asleep. My mind was too focused on the journey ahead of us. In addition, I had never flown in an airplane before. The thought of being up in the clouds was not exactly settling to me. I decided to read my little green book again to try and force all the clutter of my nervous thoughts to the back of my mind.

The Legends of Green Eagle

Interpreted by: Benito Cajero
Told by: Ta'awa Hotsko
Calabre VI

The Great Man stayed in the forest for many days thinking over what Quomvi Ta'aho had said. Finally, he decided to try and approach the people of the village his own way. He got his Soparli warriors to come with him to the edge of the tribe's village. He then walked alone out of the forest toward the village. The men of the village were the first to see him, and they brought spears and shouted at him. The Great Man raised his hands to try to show that he was coming in peace. The men of the village circled around him. He tried to speak to them, but he did not know their language. One of the villagers who seemed to be their leader came closer to the Great Man. He spoke a strange language and then he raised his spear over his head as if he was going to drive it through the

Great Man's heart. Before he could perform the act, the Soparli attacked. They made quick work of the villagers, and before the Great Man could stop them, they killed all of the warriors in the village. The women and the children were then brought out of their huts, and they mourned deeply for their dead.

The Great Man told the Soparli to gather the women and children so that they could go to the new city that he had built for them. But before they could leave, darkness filled the sky, and a voice rang through the trees: "you must complete what I have asked of you, Great Man, or you and all of your creatures shall be removed from the face of the earth." The Great Man felt very defeated; he did not want to hurt anyone. However, he had the Soparli build an enormous fire, and he told them to gather ten children from the remaining villagers. He then instructed the Soparli to throw the children into the fire. Without hesitation the Soparli obeyed the evil command. After it was finished the voice of Quomvi Ta'aho returned, "Why have you ordered the Soparli to do this thing for you? I wanted you to throw the children into the fire. Look, Great Man, look into the fire and see what I have made for you there." The Great Man turned to face the fire, and through the flames he saw the children standing there, but they were different; their skin had changed from the dark brown of the villagers to a light olive color like the Great Man's. Their faces and eyes had changed too. They looked more like those of the Great Man's. "Behold, the first ten children of your lineage. Take them and start your kingdom." Quomvi Ta'aho then spoke to the children "This is now your father; he will teach you many great things. You shall call him Dominebris, and you shall be called the Incendit, for from the fire you were born. As for you, Soparli, for your obedience you shall receive a gift. You shall have dominance over the Incendit and any of their children who may walk this earth in the future. You will be able to use your powers to hurt them without the use of brute force. You may also reward those who find favor with you." With that the children were brought out of the fire and were embraced by the Great Man. He took them back to the city he had built for them.

Brighton Bay Sanitarium
Assistant Warden Achiel Caldwell's Log
April 23, 1949

I was more than ready to go when seven o'clock rolled around this morning. We all loaded our gear and then climbed into the truck. I noticed that Custos and Mr. Pista's other servants of had added to their garb. They still wore their hooded black robes, but on their backs they had two long handles protruding in crisscross fashion from behind their heads. They also had black belts that pulled their loose robes close to their bodies. We were driven to what looked like an abandoned airfield out in the desert. There was only one plane on the airfield, and we transferred our luggage into it, while Fortis and Omnus went to the cockpit and started the plane. Once everyone was aboard we began to taxi slowly down to the north end of the runway. Then the plane turned and sat facing south. I heard what I imagined was the screaming of a banshee, as the engines fired up. Suddenly, we jolted forward and headed down the runway. The front end was the first to come off the ground and then the back end followed, and for a second we were just levitating a few inches from the ground. I then watched as the ground started to recede further and further away from where I sat. I felt my stomach become queasy, and I had to look away in order not to lose my breakfast. The next time I looked we were above the clouds, and what I could see of the ground reminded me of looking down on an anthill. The trees looked as small as my Lincoln Logs I played with as a child. The circular fields appeared to me as strange patches of grass. The cars motoring along on the road reminded me of tiny bugs marching in straight lines. Fortis stayed to fly the plane and would subsequently turn around and fly back to Natavis.

It was about four hours later when we started to descend. This was the hardest part for me. We came to the airfield we were to be landing on and circled above it twice before lining up with the landing strip and descending. I shut my eyes as the landing gear was lowered and the wheels hit the pavement. We began to bump and skid to a stop. When we came to a complete stop I could not wait to get out of that flying tin can. It was not a good first experience for me. We all grabbed our packs and proceeded to deplane.

Manus met us at the airport, and we all climbed into five army jeeps and sped off to a hotel near the edge of the town. There we met the other members of our party. There was Dr. Heinrich Toepfer, a German doctor who had been a key member of the German Resistance during World War II; Allan Abbitt, an English archeologist; and Pierre Dubois, a French explorer. Along with Dubois were three native men who came from one of the Mayan tribes living in the Yucatan jungle. Their names were Seneca, Ikal, and Kabil. We immediately entered the small hotel, which had a meeting room or dining room on the first floor. We all gathered around a table situated in the middle of the room with a map spread out on it. Pierre Dubois was the first to speak; he showed us the route we would be taking:

"We will move northwest from here. There is a dirt trail that leads about two miles into the Yucatan to the ruins of the ancient Mayan city of Muyil. There Mr. Abbitt will teach you all some of the important parts of Mayan construction so to better understand what we are looking for. After that we will have to hack our way through the jungle. Ikal and Kabil will lead the group; they know many of the native tongues as well as plants and animals living in the rainforest. They can help keep us safe on our journey."

Dubois seemed to be a likeable enough fellow, but I was struggling to focus on what he was saying due to his heavy accent. Heinrich took it from there.

"I have brought along many antidotes for some of the poisonous creatures in the rainforest, but the best way to steer clear of any issues is to avoid contact with any wildlife and to stay with the group at all times."

"In about two weeks we should be close to the area where the ancient city of Kul was supposedly located. Seneca here says that he saw the ancient city when he was a child. He will be our true guide when we get close to the area."

"The rest of today should be considered a day of rest." Dubois was again lecturing. "Try to take a few naps throughout the day if possible, as this will be the last night you will sleep in a bed for a long time."

With that the party dispersed, and we were shown to our rooms on the upper level of the hotel. The rooms were very small with only a cot-style bed in the corner under a small window. I discovered that the entire hotel was available for our use alone so we would not be disturbed.

Through the small window I saw that the hotel was not very far from what looked like a very large marketplace. I thought it might be nice to take a stroll through the streets of the lazy Mexican town. I had plenty of Pista's train stipend left over, and it seemed to be burning a hole in my pocket. I did not want to go alone, so I knocked on Ms. Peranio's door and asked her if she would be willing to come with me. She said she would be "truly thrilled" to see an authentic Mexican market, but she wanted to make sure that we were in a bigger group. We ended up asking Benson and Grant to accompany us. Benson thought it a good idea to have someone with us who could speak Spanish, so we asked Abbitt to come along. He said he was too busy at the moment making preparations, but he told us that Seneca knew enough English and he spoke fluent Spanish.

The group thought it best if I asked Seneca to join us (mostly Benson and Grant). So, as a way of proving myself, I approached him in order to ask him to come. He was sitting on the ground with Ikal and Kabil when I found him. He was much bigger than the other two natives. He wore a wrapped cloth over his thighs and upper legs. The sides were slit to help with mobility. His upper body was naked, and you could see every muscle flex and move as he turned to look at me. He had what appeared to be a piece of bone pierced through his nose. His hair was tied up in a knot on top of his head. He had wrist bands and leg bands decorated with colorful beads. There was a gruesome scar down his left cheek and a strange tattoo of skulls protruded past the cloth on his right leg. I asked him, somewhat timidly, if he would like to join us as we roamed the marketplace. He looked me up and down and said something in Spanish to the other two that made them chuckle. Then he turned back to me and nodded. Somehow I thought it was going to take more convincing than that, but he followed me over to the others, and the five of us walked into the marketplace.

We must have stuck out like a sore thumb, because upon entering the market every vendor started to yell at us and throw up their most intricate and beautiful bobbles. We walked very slowly, taking in all of the sites. We stopped so Benson could buy a very elaborate knife. Seneca told Benson that the vendor said the knife was used by a priest to sacrifice humans to the sun god and that the knife itself held the spirits of those it had killed. Benson snickered to himself, but he bought the thing anyway, paying $2.00 for it. Then we moved on. Grant found a poncho that had an eagle sewn on it. He wanted to buy it, but he also wanted to haggle on the price. Seneca said that the vendor wanted $5.00 American. Grant told him that he would pay no more than $3.50. The vendor said he would not sell, but Seneca lifted his cloth on his right leg and spoke rather coarsely to the vendor in Spanish. He then turned to Grant and said, "He take your price."

Towards the end of the market area we saw a shop where a little girl stood out front, holding up a traditional Mayan dress. It exposed the shoulders and was embroidered with beautiful pink and red flowers over the chest. The skirt was dyed red while the upper half was white under the embroidery. Ms. Peranio called the dress "simply lovely", and the three of us men implored her to go in and try it on. She did so, and when she came back out from the little shop into the sun she looked like a Mayan goddess. It fit very nicely in all the right places (if I might be so bold). We all complimented her, and even Seneca, who had seemed disinterested in the trip thus far took notice of her beauty. Ms. Peranio simply beamed with happiness, and she eagerly paid the little girl $10.00 for it. Seneca told her she had paid the little girl too much, but Ms. Peranio simply said, "She needs the money for her family more than I do." Seneca put on an angry face, but he did not make any move toward the little girl.

I suddenly realized that we had spent far more time wandering around the market than I planned on doing.

After commenting that it was past time for us to return, I suggested we hed back. Together we turned around and headed back up toward our hotel. The sun was beginning to set as we walked past one booth that seemed to be selling relics and artifacts. It was there that something caught my eye. It was a necklace with a palm-sized rock dangling from it. On the rock was a four-part diagram. I bent down to look closer and sure enough: it looked like the diagram I had seen in Patronis's room that night in the sanitarium. The only difference was that the words on this one were written in a different language. I assumed it was Mayan. I asked Seneca to inquire how much this rock was. He stared at me funny for a second and then he said, "You want to buy necklace?" I think he thought I was crazy. I told him it was special. He shook his head and then asked how much it was. Seneca and the merchant talked for quite some time before Seneca turned to me and with a furrowed brow said, "Man says necklace is sacred; he keeps for himself." I was instantly very interested. Even though it had been I who wanted to return to the hotel, I asked Seneca to have the merchant to expound on the rock. Seneca debated with the man some more about the rock and then looked at me and said, "His father found the rock in the jungle many years ago. It is a family heirloom." I knew what I had to do. I walked over to the merchant and showed him the diagram. I pointed to each picture and said, "Strix, Sapator, Soparli, Syreni." He looked at me with wide eyes and then slowly backed away. I said to Seneca, "Tell him I've come from far away to bring an end to these legends." Seneca looked at me strangely but then conveyed the message. The vendor got down on his knees and made the sign of the cross and spoke to Seneca, who turned to me and said with a sort of unbelief "He say take rock." I smiled, but when I looked at the rest of my party, they did not understand. I put the rock in my pocket and told the group to keep moving. They did as I asked, but none of them took their eyes off of me. I threw ten dollars on the man's stand before moving away.

I could tell the group had questions. Finally, Mattie spoke up: "I know everyone is thinking what I'm about to say, so what's with the rock?"

I worked to keep my explanation simple. "It is a rock with a diagram from *the Legends of Green Eagle* on it. These are the animals that served the Great Man in the book."

"Yes," Benson stated, "but those are just fairy tales; they have nothing to do with reality. Why did that vendor back away from you that way? This rock meant more to him than just some story in a book for children."

"I'm beginning to think that Patronis and this whole event are somehow connected to *the Legends of Green Eagle Fables.*" I was trying to be patient with his attitude.

I looked back and saw that all three of them had stopped walking and were looking at me like I was crazy. My mind rewound to what Pista had said, "Don't be afraid to open your eyes on this journey, even though the social norms and your companions may look down upon that."

When I returned to my hotel room it dawned on me that it was happening! I was becoming like Patronis! For a moment I felt better about my situation. Maybe I could apprehend Patronis; maybe this would work. If I could think like Patronis, perhaps I could catch him at his own game.

The Legends of Green Eagle

Interpreted by: Benito Cajero
Told by: Ta'awa Hotsko
Calabre VII

Dominebris spent many years teaching the young ones how to build, how to farm and how to hunt. He taught them how to count and how to write; he even began a certain type of currency and taught them how to use it. He came to view these little children as his beloved ones. They took a lot of his time. His favorite little one he named Colel; she was beautiful, with her tan skin and jet-black hair that matched her eyes. She was beautiful. Dominebris loved to take Colel on walks through the forest and talk to her about nature.

After many moons the Soparli became jealous. They began to despise Dominebris for spending so much time with his new humans. There was one Soparli, named Tapani, who stirred the others into anger. He coaxed the other Soparli into taking action against Dominebris. One day as Dominebris and Colel were walking through the forest, the Soparli intervened and took Colel as their prisoner. Dominebris became furious and called out to Quomvi-Ta'aho for help, but there was no answer. Finally he decided to go and talk to the Soparli to see if he could get Colel back. He traveled to their city and met Tapani there. He pleaded with Tapani for Colel, but Tapani refused. The other Soparli who had been told that Dominebris was heartless saw how their father was still a passionate being. They talked Tapani into releasing Colel. Tapani finally compromised. "We will give your prized possession back to you if you promise to give us full control over the Incendit and their kind. Dominebris could think of nothing but the safety of Colel, and so he agreed to the terms. That was the day that the Soparli gained control over humankind.

Brighton Bay Sanitarium
Assistant Warden Achiel Caldwell's Log
April 24, 1949

I was awakened early in the morning by a heavy pounding on my door. When I drowsily turned my lamp on I noticed smoke creeping under the door. Then the door was shattered into about four pieces. There stood Custos. "Come, we must leave," he thundered as he grabbed me and practically carried me out of the room. Black smoke was billowing down the hallways. Pushing down the stairs, we saw the flames. They were licking at the ceiling in the dining room, and no one was attempting to put them out.

The out-of-control flames were now at a point where they could not be tamed. I knew then that we all had to get out, because the place was going to burn to the ground. We hustled outside where we met Grant, Maddie and Benson. A bit later, Dr. Toepfer, Abbitt and Dubois showed up with the native guides. Our guides actually saved all of our packs and supplies for the journey. Abbitt was somewhat perturbed, because the map for the trip had been in the dining room and now was completely obliterated by the fire. It was about fifteen minutes later that Omnus, Custos, Mendax and Procul all showed up. Out of breath, they nonetheless gathered us together and spoke quickly.

They said that there had been an attempt to sabotage our mission, and once the townspeople found out they would be very angry with us. Custos said we should leave now and be on our way so as to not cause a scene. Abbitt and Dubois agreed, and we all slipped away into the jungle as the first bells started to ring alerting the town to the burning building. We had not gone very far before we all stopped to change into our hiking gear, seeing as we were all still in our night clothes. Once we had all changed, we walked the three miles down the dirt path in almost complete silence. The jungle around us seemed to grow ever denser, and with it the darkness caused by the menacing jungle trees. The sun had not yet risen, yet the air was still muggy, and I was perspiring heavily by the time we reached Muyil. The sky was stained a pink color, and the jungle seemed to be coming to life. Tropical birds sang of the coming morning, and monkeys cried out to their fellow tree dwellers that there were trespassers nearby. The first rays of the sun gave shape to the beauty of the ancient Mayan city. In the center rose what looked like a pyramid, but instead of being triangular in shape, this was more like a square with layers. There was a steep set of stairs that rose all the way to the top of the tower. Abbitt began to explain.

"This is an ancient Mayan palace. It pales in comparison to some of the other palaces found throughout the Yucatan, but it is nonetheless a good example of what we might be looking for in the jungle. The Mayans made this structure using mostly limestone. Laborers would haul the rock by hand from the quarry and distribute it at this work site. The innards of this palace were mostly just limestone rubble, but the outer layer had been neatly planned in order to give a royal appearance and a sense of unbelievable craftsmanship." Abbitt was warming to his subject, "The Mayans built these structures using their own mathematical system that went along with their own form of writing. They were very advanced for their time period. Then, all of a sudden, the Mayans abandoned their cities and went to live in villages or other places throughout Mexico. No one has ever figured out exactly why these cities were abandoned, but there have been many theories that suggest their motives might have been lack of basic resources such as food and clothing."

"We are going deep into the forest," Abbitt continued, "and there are certain general signs that we may be close to a Mayan Plaza. First, there are almost always stone markers marking out the corners of the plaza. The markers were used as signs to alert people that they were close to a Mayan city. Another indicator would be a large clearing in the trees. Many Mayan plazas were built in a clearing, but in our instance, the trees most likely were cleared from the area. Another dead giveaway is a rise or elevation to the ground. Many plazas were built up off the canopy floor of the jungle. One reason for this was the sandy ground of the rain forest. It would have affected the integrity of the buildings over time, causing the foundations to crack and crumble. With a layer of limestone as a buffer between the ground and the structure, the Mayan temples and palaces would have solid foundations for centuries to come. The other reason for building on an elevation was that the Mayans believed in a sun god who was all-powerful. They built upward in order to be closer to him and show their own power in doing so."

It was obvious Abbitt was enjoying his role. But just then he proceeded to walk up the stairway of the palace. We all followed. It was not easy, because the steps were steep and very narrow. I had to climb almost sideways so as not to lose my balance. It was a long way up, but when I got to the top the view was spectacular. Ahead of me the rest of the plaza was spread out. I could see huts and another building with a set of sloping stairs that I assumed was a temple. I walked under a covered passageway to the other side of the palace. This view faced a crystal blue lagoon; most likely the Mayans who lived here were fishermen first. It made me wonder about what Abbitt had said concerning the theories of why they abandoned their plazas. That lagoon was probably crawling with fish and crabs - plenty of food for a small city to survive on, not to mention any crops that the Mayans grew on the side or animals they could hunt in the jungle. It just did not make sense to me how an early people group who could build unbelievable structures like this one would leave them because they could not figure out how to get food. We climbed back down the palace stairs and walked over to the temple. Abbitt spoke again.

"Another way to recognize Mayan ruins is to look for a temple building. These buildings are more oblong and have a set of stairs usually leading up. As you can see here, this temple also has an altar where the priest might make sacrifices to the gods.

Now that I've given you some signs to look for when we are searching for the Mayan city of Kul, it is time to start our trek through the jungle. Mr. Dubois, do you want to give us some guidelines before we begin?"

"Yes, it is urgently important to remember that we are entering a very wild and dangerous rainforest. There are thousands of things in there that could cause you harm, and many more things that are even unknown to mankind. It is important that we always stay together, so no leaving the group to go exploring." Dubois was looking at each of us in turn. "Ikal and Kabil will be blazing a path for us, so it would be wise to stay upon the path. Both of these men also know the tribes that live in the rainforest. We are not going to be able to head in a straight line toward our destination, because we are trying to stay out of certain tribes' hunting grounds. We also need to stay somewhat quiet. Who knows what predator a loud noise or two could bring our way? I suggest any weapons you were issued be kept ready at all times. So, now that we've established some guidelines, let's get going, shall we."

With that, we all walked to the northwest edge of the plaza. I stared ahead at the vast tree line that stood almost like a solid ten-foot high wall in front of me. I was already dreading the idea of going into this never-ending forest, but I ground my teeth and clenched my fists to strengthen my resolve. Somewhere in there Patronis might be waiting for us. I looked to my side. Dubois was checking his compass beside Dr. Toepfer, who was inventorying his medical bag. Ikal and Kabil had taken out some rather nasty looking machetes and were swinging them around, presumably warming up their shoulders for the constant hacking motion that they would be doing. Custos looked at the forest as if he were searching it for animals. His compatriots were talking quietly behind him. It was very strange, all of these men had the same cloaks on that must have made them hot as blazes. Yet, Mendax had pale skin, while Omnus and Manus looked Arabian, Procul was clearly Asian and of course Custos was very dark like an African. They were all from different backgrounds but they clearly had a great connection through Pista.

Grant and Benson were chatting with Abbitt. They appeared to be asking a question about the architecture of the palace. Seneca stood on the far end of the line next to Ms. Peranio (who looked somewhat worried as she studied the line of massive trees). Seneca was wielding a huge, yet crudely constructed axe. The blade seemed to be made of stone. He held it against his shoulder to support its massive weight. The company seemed ready to traverse the rain-forest. It was not quite noon yet by my watch, yet the sun blazed down an intense heat, intensified by the humidity that seemed to cling to the air, almost suffocating our bodies. We had filled our canteens the night before with well water from the town of Tulum. I took a swig quickly as the sweat seemed to weep from every inch of my body. I felt like a washcloth being rung out in the sink. The time had come. Both Kabil and Ikal took up their positions in the front of the line, hacking at the foliage of the rainforest. Dubois followed closely behind them, and he was followed by Manus and Omnus. After them, Abbitt went with Grant, Benson and Ms. Peranio. Then came Custos and me, followed by Dr. Toepfer, Mendax, Procul and finally, bringing up the rear of our little exploration group, came Seneca. The path we tread was somewhat easy at first, and we seemed to be making good time. There were little trails leading through the area around Muyil, probably made by some tourists who felt the need to attempt walking into the rainforest.

We had gone a couple of miles when Ikal and Kabil moved to their right and began to cut a new path away from any of the remaining small rabbit trails. The going got immensely tougher after that point, and before I knew it, I looked up and saw that the sun had sunk lower than the trees. It was starting to get dark in the forest when

Dubois held his hand up and we all halted. He walked back down the line whispering, "We are going to set up camp here." The lot of us felt somewhat unsure of what that entailed, but everyone else, even Custos and his companions, burst into action as we watched. Kabil, Ikal and Seneca all started slashing the foliage in a circular pattern around the group. Custos and Mendax began to scour the area for wood suitable for a fire. Omnus, Manus and Procul created a triangle of guards around the perimeter. They all took out their blades they were carrying. They resembled the traditional Samurai Sword to me, with the curvature in the blade itself. But these swords were extraordinary; they seemed to glow an odd bluish-silver color. They actually lit up the dark jungle around them. Everyone seemed to stop what they were doing for a moment and stare in a stupefied fashion at the amazing glowing weapons. Custos and the other men did not seem to notice or care about the attention they were getting. Grant finally got up the courage to go ask Custos about the swords. It turns out these swords were Pista's great technological inventiona. They collected the power from the sun through their handles and pushed that heat into the blade. The blade was white-hot, which made it glow in the darkness.

Abbitt and Dr. Toepfer began to set up their tents. Dubois went off from the group to scout ahead a bit. Dr. Toepfer called the four of us over and showed us how to set up our own tents, demonstrating how to use our mosquito nets as a type of barrier over our tent as an extra layer of protection against bugs. He told us to take all of our belongings inside the tent, so as not to attract any unwanted predators that may steal whatever they could.

After everything had been set up, we started a fire and sat down to a meal that was provided by Ikal and Kabil. They produced a medium-size pot that had been crammed full of dried meat. Although I had no idea what kind of animal this mystery meat came from, I ate it without hesitation; I was famished.

Dubois had found a small stream up ahead, and he made three trips to and from the stream with a pot. We boiled the water on the fire and then refilled our canteens. Dubois and the doctor had brought about six extra canteens in order to keep an extra supply of fresh water at the ready. I put some salve on my toe before going to sleep. The pain was very intense from all the hiking we had done.

That night, Dubois set up a night watch system where two people at a time would be responsible for guarding the rest of the sleeping party. Each couple was responsible for two hours of time before they could wake their relief team. Dubois then split us off into partners. I was paired with Custos. Grant got to watch with Ms. Peranio, which made me somewhat jealous of my situation. With everything now settled, we went off to bed for the night. I slept hard, even though the ground was uneven. I was awakened around three by Seneca, who had had the watch before mine. I walked out of my tent to complete darkness; the fire had died down to ashes and neither the moon nor the stars' light could penetrate the thick Yucatan canopy. It was eerily silent in the forest as well. It was as if the rainforest was under the effect of the bewitching hour. Or was it because something was close to our camp watching us? I shivered at the thought of being watched. It was then I sensed Custos was standing directly next to me. It took every muscle in my body not to let out a scream; instead, I made a muffled whimper. "Don't sneak up on me like that, Custos." He apologized and grabbed a few sticks to restart the fire. The warm glow soon turned into a small blaze that lit up the trees around us and made them look as if they were dancing. It was quiet for a long while, but he finally spoke.

"I heard tell that you found a strange rock in the marketplace in Muyil yesterday. May I see it?"

I touched the necklace I had around my neck. I had forgotten it was there until Custos mentioned it. I took the stone off of the cord. The night I bought the stone I had found that the stone itself had no hole where the cord of the necklace could loop through it. Rather, there a sort of strong magnet that kept it clasped to the cord. This means the rock was highly magnetic.

I looked at the rock as it sat in my dirty hand. Sighing, I gave it over to Custos who examined the markings closely. "This will only bring you trouble," he said as he dropped the rock back into my palm. Then I quickly reclasped the rock to the cord and tucked it into my shirt for safe keeping. I acted as though he had said nothing; I didn't want to bring any attention to the necklace so I did not have to answer any questions.

"I have not seen those marks in years. Do you know what they mean?"

I was taken aback; he knew about the diagram! It scared me slightly, and I decided it would be necessary to lie to get information out of him.

"No, I was just drawn to it by the elaborate drawings. It seems to me to be a very authentic Mayan artwork. Am I right?"

It was clear that Custos was excited.

"Yes, you are right. This is part of the Mayan writing that describes their origins. You see, some of them believed in four different deities that were all at war with one another."

"You mean like factions," I asked. "Fighting one another for ultimate power and prowess?"

"Yeah, sort of like that. The Mayans believed that these gods would protect them and care for their people. Except the different deities needed each other in order to maintain their power. The Mayans believed that these gods would protect them and care for their people to the end of time."

"What happened? I mean, where were these gods when the Mayans were evacuating their towns?"

"They had become arrogant with power. They were too proud to care for the people who needed them the most. They had forgotten their duty to those who served them."

Custos looked very downhearted as he shared these pieces of history. He stared straight into the slowly dying fire. I could see the flames dance in the glare from his eyes. Did this make him sad for some reason, or was he just tired? Either way I did not push the issue, and for the remainder of my time outside, I sat watching the fire with him. I did not hear a single sound come from the vast jungle around me during the entire time I was on duty. Silence is definitely more unnerving than unfamiliar sounds.

Brighton Bay Sanitarium
Assistant Warden Achiel Caldwell's Log
April 25, 1949

It was raining quite heavily all morning. We began to clean up camp at daybreak. As we were doing so, Grant found a moderately large snake coiled up under his tent. He froze for a moment and whispered to Seneca, who immediately came over and with one swift hacking motion of the machete, cut off the snake's head. The snake's body writhed upon the ground for a few seconds, before finally becoming rigid with death. Seneca picked up the back half of the snake and threw it over his large shoulder. "Make good meal," he said while rubbing his belly.

The rain subsided as we continued at a solid pace for about five hours, until Ikal called for everyone to halt. Then he, Kibal and Dubois seemed to be having a conference at the front of the line. Ms. Peranio became uncomfortable with the stoppage.

"Why are they stopping? What's going on? Seneca, please go check to see what the problem is up there." Immediately Ms. Peranio blushed. I think it was due to her realization of how demanding she sounded.

Seneca made his way past us to the front and began to debate with members of the group. After a few moments he came back.

"We near hunting grounds of Ixil. Very dangerous people."

"Well isn't that swell! We are already in a pickle; I knew I should have stayed home." Ms. Peranio was decidedly not happy.

"Calm down, Ms. Peranio," Custos directed her. "I'm sure our guide has everything under control."

"Yeah, you're probably right." Ms. Peranio attempted a dim smile. "I just hope we can go around this area without...."

Before she could finish we heard some crashing and yelling coming from ahead of us. Dubois signaled for us to get down, and we all fell to our knees. We then heard splashing and then the sounds of what could only be men dying. There was the whoosh of an arrow maybe once or twice and then the sounds of the fighting seemed to move further off into the jungle. We must have waited there for about five minutes before Dubois sent Ikal to scout ahead and figure out what was happening. After another ten minutes Ikal returned and spoke softly to Kibal and Dubois. Then Dubois raised his hand, and we all straightened up again and began to move forward.

Ikal led us out into an open field where a beautiful stream rushed past us. Beside the stream on the ground were five to seven bodies. There were body parts lying around completely disassociated from one another. It was obvious that several bodies were missing limbs. Some seriously suffering people were still alive but had blood pouring out in all directions, like little streams coursing their paths in the sand. I had never seen the effects of warfare, but it seemed even more savage to see it in the middle of this impenetrable jungle, where the hands of time had not affected the natives. It was almost as if I had stepped into a time machine and gone back a thousand years to find this battle. The worst part about it was that some of these so-called "warriors" were only boys who looked to be thirteen years old at best. Everyone hung their heads, and Ms. Peranio began to cry. Just then, there was a rustle coming from the tall grass. Seneca raised his battle axe but lowered it again when he saw a small boy no older than eight stumbling out into the grass. He had an arrow stuck over his collarbone. He was obviously in shock as he stared at the odd procession that stood in front of him. He began to sway and started to fall, but Custos caught him. Ms. Peranio and Dr. Toepfer ran to take a closer look at the young boy.

"Check the rest of his body, Ms. Peranio." We all were treated to the professional side of Dr. Toepfer. "All right, the boy is fortunate that the arrow went straight through."

"Check the arrow for poison, Dr. Toepfer; he may be beyond our help." It would never have occurred to me to do this, and I was grateful for Dubois for his insight.

"There is no poison on this arrow. I think he's going to be okay," Dr. Toepfer confirmed.

"The boy has sustained no other wounds, Doctor." The two were working well as a team.

"We must keep going. Leave the boy."

"He's right, Hienrich," said Dubois. "We have to keep moving. We are unsafe and unprotected out here in the open. These tribal battles are short, but eall too soon the triumphant warriors come looking for trophies.

"Trophies? I dare say, what trophies could they possibly get from these poor small boys lying here?" asked Abbitt.

Seneca grabbed Mr. Abbitt's hand and pretended to cut his thumb off, and then he pointed at the man's foot. Seneca then proceeded to take his battle axe and point it at his own neck making a clucking noise for effect. There was a moment of stunned silence.

Mr. Abbitt gulped, "How ghastly!"

Dubois elaborated, "Yes, these tribes like to wear the hair of their dead enemies on their clothes as a trophy. The heads are taken, put on spikes and displayed around their tribes as a warning to others."

"Ms. Peranio, leave him," Seneca ordered.

"SENECA! You will wait one minute while the doctor and I take the arrow out of him, or you can go off with your native friends by yourself."

We all raised our eyebrows at her as she put the big native in his place. He wore a scowl on his face as he kept staring at her and the doctor. The doctor took a sharp pair of scissors from his medical bag and had Ms. Peranio hold the arrow on both sides of the shoulder while he snipped off the barbed end of the arrow. Then Ms. Peranio held the boy up while Dr. Toepfer pulled the rest of the arrow out of the entry point. The boy let out a soft moan as the arrow came sliding out. The flow of blood from the wound had pooled on top of the protruding collar bone. Dr. Toepfer quickly wrapped clean linens around the gash and tied them on the backside of the shoulder. Then he helped Ms. Peranio sling the young boy over her shoulder and we set off once again, this time at a brisk pace. Once we were back in the jungle I offered to carry the boy for Ms. Peranio. She thanked me as I slung him over my own shoulder. He was very light; not like an 8-year-old from the States. We got about a half mile into the jungle again before the boy woke up and began to thrash around violently on my back. He even whacked me on the neck once or twice, but I ignored him. It was only when he began to scream that Seneca came close, grabbed him by the hair, and told him something in a foreign tongue. The boy looked with wide eyes at Custos and Mendax as they walked closely behind him. Whatever he said seemed to work; the boy was silent the rest of the day.

As the sun was going down that night we did the same thing as the night before. We set up camp and ate from our supplies of dehydrated meat and fruit. We gave some food to the boy, but he seemed to be terrified of us. I heard Ms. Peranio walk over to Seneca and ask him what he had said to the poor boy to make him so afraid of us.

"He be quiet or gods kill him."

Ms. Peranio looked disgustedly at Seneca, but the big brute just smiled back at her. The boy seemed to stay as far away from Pista's men as he could. I found his behavior a bit strange. That night we switched up the watch and I was given the night off. I applied the salve again to my toe. Tonight, the pain was more like a dull ache. This must be some strong salve that I slept even better than the night before, but before I drifted off, I read from my leather-bound book.

The Legends of Green Eagle
Interpreted by: Benito Cajero
Told by: Ta'awa Hotsko
Calabre VIII

"Dominebris spent many years teaching the young ones how to build, how to farm and how to hunt. He taught them how to count and how to write; he even came up with a certain type of currency and taught them how to use it. After all the Incendit had grown they began to have their own children, and in turn they taught their children. Dominebris watched as a society began to emerge in the beautiful city he had built them. Soon the number of people in the city was great. The city needed to be expanded, but instead of expanding, Dominebris took his Sapator and went off in search of a new place to build a city. While searching, Dominebris got lost in the vast forest. Out of desperation he cried out to Quomvi Ta'aho, "Oh Great One, I cannot see where I am going. I wish to have eyes that can go above the trees and search the forest from above in order to find a place to build a second great city." A voice that sounded like the creaking of the trees in the wind responded. "I once promised you that I would give you four animals who would serve you. I will fulfill my promise, although you will not seem to do what I have asked of you. I give you these owls as your servants. You shall call them 'Strix'; they shall be your eyes in the great open sky. They will judge the deeds of all from on high. The Strix will be a rival to the other sects and will ultimately cause you and your kingdom great pain and suffering." Now I have completed my vow unto you, Dominebris. If you seek further favor with me, you must bring me sacrifices. At that moment, a beautiful creature fluttered down from the trees and stood in front of Dominebris. She had the most beautiful blond hair and light blue eyes. She bowed low and handed Dominebris a great horn, made from the horn of a ram. "This is Siibil, blow it whenever you need the help of your faithful servants of the sky," she said. "What shall I do for you, Master?" Dominebris sent her to go and find a good place where the next city would be built. She came back and told Dominebris of a small plateau that had a good vantage point of the land around it. When Dominebris got to the place, he knew it was the perfect spot to build his capitol city. He would call it Certuitu, for from it the surrounding land was in clear sight.

Brighton Bay Sanitarium
Assistant Warden Achiel Caldwell's Log
April 26, 1949

I was awakened by Ms. Peranio's screams at dawn the following morning. I quickly got dressed and ran as fast as my sore legs could go to her tent. By the time I had arrived, a small crowd had already gathered, but it did not seem as if anyone was moving to help Ms. Peranio. I pushed through the gathered onlookers and saw a long-legged black spider the size of a man's hand sitting on the mosquito netting in front of Mattie's tent. She was inside the tent almost in a fetal position in the furthest corner. Her eyes were fixed in horror upon the large spider. I looked at Seneca, who began to laugh. "Is it poisonous?" I asked. Seneca shook his head no, but he did not stop laughing. I took my hand and slapped the spider off the tent cover. Then I got down on my hands and knees and asked Mattie whether she was all right. She seemed to be trying to calm down. "I have a deathly fear of spiders," she admitted in a hoarse voice. "Well it's gone now. You can come out; it's safe," I reassured her and looked at the others. Grant had a strange smile on his face. Benson simply shook his head as he walked away. Ms. Peranio stuck her head out of the tent, doing a double check of the area to make sure the thing had not come back. Then she exited the tent and began to pick up her belongings.

I went back to my tent to take it down, but my eyes caught sight of the boy we had helped the day before. He had been tied to a tree. I called Dubois over to take a look at him, trying not to make a huge fuss about the situation (I knew Mattie would be furious if she saw the boy tied up like this). He came over and began to untie the poor boy. "He tried to escape twice last night; Seneca finally had to gag him and tie him to this tree," Dubois explained. I knew if this kept up, we would never make it to our destination, so I decided to call a short meeting with Dubois, Benson, Abbitt and Dr. Toepfer.

"We can't have this boy running off every night or giving away our position to any of his native friends," I opened the meeting with my concern.

"I thought it foolish to bring the boy in the first place," Benson sputtered. "Blame it on the woman's softened sense of pity. This boy could most definitely be the death of us all."

Dubois added, "Seneca tells me this boy is from the Q'eqchi tribe. If he is correct, that tribe lies directly in our path toward Kul. This boy actually could be our good luck charm. If we deliver him to his people healthy and in one piece, they may let us go through their lands."

Abbitt chimed in. "I think it would be a rather enlightening journey to witness how a native village operates. I say we give it a go."

"You did hear him say the word 'Maybe,' right? That means there is a chance that they slaughter us and take our scalps as trophies," Benson scoffed.

"I agree with Benson," Toepfer said. "I don't like the odds of this mission. I say we let the boy go and continue on our way."

"There is also a slight problem with that train of thought, Doctor. If we simply let him go, he could go to his village and tell them about us, then circle back and track us down and kill us." Dubois's comment served as a good reminder to me.

I wanted the meeting to come to an end. "The odds here seem to be stacked against us either way. I say the only true way to settle this issue is to do so by democratic vote with the entire group."

All those involved in the short meeting agreed, and we gathered everyone together in the center of our man-made clearing and told them of the situation and the choices we had. The boy stood behind the circle looking worriedly at us all. We had to wait for Dubois to explain it to Ikal, Kibal, and Seneca, and then we voted. It was very close with Seneca, Dr. Toepfer, Grant, Benson, Ikal, Kibal and Procul voting to let him go. Dubois, Peranio, Abbitt, Custos, Omnus, Manus, Mendax and I voted to take the boy back to his tribe. The yeas had won by the slim margin of eight to seven. We told Seneca to talk to the boy and inform him of our decision. It was not until I had already voted that I realized we were putting a lot of faith into this little boy to first, lead us back to his tribe, and not turn his tribe against us, all the while not running away and leaving us stranded, off course in the vast jungle. I felt that I might have made the wrong decision; it felt even worse knowing that my vote might have been the deciding vote as well.

We packed up rather quickly, seeing as we had wasted some time trying to make our decision. The rest of the day was spent following the young boy who was taking us; after all, our map had been burned in the fire at the inn. Once we had truly entered the forest, we had been using the compass and the memory of Ikal and Kibal. According to my compass we had been heading in more of a straight northern direction. It was encouraging to me when by mid-day the boy stumbled upon an old hunting path that his tribe had used in the past. The little trail made for quicker movement, but it also meant that we had entered Q'eqchi lands. We moved on until dusk and found ourselves on a little rise looking down into a valley. The boy pointed down into the valley, and as I looked closer I saw a plume of smoke rising from the jungle. I assumed that he was telling Seneca that that was his village. Seneca became somewhat animated in his conversations with the boy. He finally broke away and went to talk to Dubois. Dubois seemed to hang his head with whatever Seneca told him. We then listened as Dubois told the group what the boy had said.

"The boy says that the smoke is not from his village, but rather it is originating from a large Ixil hunting party. He thinks that the hunting party is going to take out his village tomorrow and that this is the group of Ixil warriors that ambushed him and his people a day ago. He says there are about thirty warriors involved and most of them are experienced warriors as well; not like the boys we found by the stream the other day." Dubois sighed. "We only have one choice in my opinion. We've come this far and we have to try to stop these men from capturing and killing our only safe passage through these lands. Here is my suggestion: We stay here tonight without fires in order to conceal our location. Then in the morning, before the sun rises, those who are willing should come with me and the boy and try to make a stand against the Ixil, maybe taking them by surprise before they can move off. I know it sounds insane; I am willing to listen to any other suggestions."

But there were none; everyone had their heads down. I don't think anyone liked the situation we were in, but it seemed everyone had to come to terms with the grim reality. Finally, Dubois asked for volunteers to fight tomorrow. Custos, Mendax, Manus, and Omnus all volunteered. Then Seneca, Ikal and Kibal all walked forward and said they would go with Dubois. Dubois seemed pleased with this number, but before he could close the impromptu meeting, Benson and Dr. Toepfer volunteered as well.

Then from the deepest part of me came a stirring the likes of which I had never imagined would originate from me. Before I could stop myself, I said, "I would like to come too." Everyone stared at me as if I were on fire. I don't think anyone expected me to speak up. I instantly regretted my decision. What did I know about warfare? Nevertheless, I had made my choice and the group was forced to accept it.

That night there was very little sleep for anyone. The plan had been determined and all agreed. The warring party would surround the Ixil before dawn and the rest of our group would move west, following another hunting path that led to an abandoned village, where they would wait for the rest of the party. Hopefully we would all meet up at the village and be able to travel the rest of the short distance to the Q'eqchi village together. I felt sick to my stomach. I could just picture myself lying in this god-forsaken jungle with a gaping wound from an Ixil spear, my life-blood rushing from me just like the young boys we had seen next to the stream. *What would my last moments feel like* I wondered? *What would the cross-over feel like? Would there be anything on the other side?* I shuddered to think about it. Luckily Ms. Peranio came over to distract me.

"Hello, Ace, how are you feeling?"

"Oh. I'm all right I guess, just thinking about tomorrow."

"I just wanted to tell you that I think it was very brave of you to want to go with the warring party. I know that some people have given you grief because Dr. Ambridge and Pista put you in charge. I think you showed leadership qualities today, wanting to go into action to protect the rest of us who aren't fighting. I know you might feel scared right now, but you put your best foot forward by volunteering today."

"Thank you, Mattie," I was somewhat tongue-tied.

Mattie added, "I'll be saying a special prayer for you tonight as well."

I didn't know how to respond to that. As she walked away there was a false sense of joy that covered my fear like a thin blanket on a deathly cold night. That one kind word from a beautiful woman would not be enough to help me sleep this night. It did help to know that Ms. Peranio was thinking of me. I knew my only option tonight would be to read to calm my nerves. Thus, I picked up my green leather-bound book and began to pour over its pages once again.

The Legends of Green Eagle
Interpreted by: Benito Cajero
Told by: Ta'awa Hotsko
Calabre IX

The time came when all the Incendit had grown old. They became grandparents to a much larger generation. Dominebris still walked amongst his people, but not as often. Many of the young ones did not know him other than he was their father and leader. Many of the youths started to bow when he approached, as if he were their king. The Great Man did not appreciate the gesture. He began to seek refuge with his Soparli, who lived separately from the humans. He enjoyed their company for some time. Then news came from the city of the Incendit that four of the First Children had died. The city was thrown into a panic; they did not know what to do or who would lead them when the Incendit were all gone. So the people sent messengers to find Dominebris in order to have him come and lead them. By the time Dominebris got back to the city it was a war zone. The rest of the Incendit were either too sick or too old to lead the people anymore, and the younger generations had turned on each other, grouping off into family factions. Dominebris had to call upon the Strix to put an end to the bloodshed within the city. He then called a meeting of the leaders of the family factions in order to try to return peace to the people. At the meeting, the Great Man could not speak over the warring talk of the faction leaders. Finally, Dominebris came up with a plan that was suitable for all the faction leaders. He told them that he and the

Sapator would help the families build their own cities. The city of the Incendit would be the holy city, where the ten Incendit would be buried. The Soparli would guard the city and become its main inhabitants. The next years were spent separating the forest land into separate pieces for the ten new kingdoms of the Incendit to inhabit and then helping the factions to build their great cities. Dominebris began to feel more like a pawn then the great, reverent father figure he was supposed to be. Towards the end of the construction of the ten cities, Dominebris once again wandered off into the forest to be alone.

Brighton Bay Sanitarium
Assistant Warden Achiel Caldwell's Log
April 27, 1949

I must have dozed off at some point in the night, because it was still dark when I felt a strong arm shake me awake. Custos put his finger over his mouth as he summoned me to come with him. We made our way to the center of the camp, where the rest of the group stood ready. I was given a machete and a flare gun, Dubois and Dr. Toepfer both had long rifles. Custos and the rest of Pista's laborers had their long curved knives drawn, Benson had a machete, pistol and a shotgun, and Ikal and Kibal had small axes and spears in their hands. But Seneca stuck out as he had the huge battle axe slung over his shoulder. The boy carried nothing but a bow and arrow. We slowly made our way through the dark jungle, using only the blue glow of the swords to meander our way towards the camp. As we drew near the dimly lit fires of the Ixil party became visible. We sent Ikal and Omnus ahead to take care of any outposts on watch. They returned within the hour saying they only found two men on watch. A plan was formulated quite quickly. Seneca and the boy would lead a party from the right side and Dubois and Benson would lead a small group from the left. The doctor, Custos, Ikal and I would be sent behind the camp to stop any of the men from escaping. I watched in awe as Omnus and Mendax seemed to climb up two palm trees with ease. We were to give the signal of an owl hoot when we got into position. Custos led the doctor and me to the back of the camp. He motioned for the three of us to spread out, but then he came and stood by me.

"Do not worry, Achiel; no harm will befall you." It would have been reassuring had he said it a day or even an hour before now, but I had no time to be grateful for his comment, because as soon as he said it, he gave the call of an owl. Instantly, action and chaos ensued.

Over at the head of the camp I could see the trees moving and then all of a sudden, Omnus and Mendax appeared jumping out of the trees and easily chopping the heads off of a few of the Ixil warriors who had gathered to investigate. Dubois and Seneca stomped into the clearing, yelling as if there were ten of them. From the ground rose the bodies of sleeping men, their outlines growing to immense size in the firelight. The sun was just starting to turn the sky reddish pink and the light from it made the natives look all the more menacing. Dubois fired his rifle, knocking one warrior off his feet. Another shot was fired from the right, and another native fell. I watched as Seneca ran at a group of five natives, the small boy at his side. The boy took aim and shot his arrow with amazing accuracy, sending the arrow through one of the enemy's eye sockets; he instantly fell - lifeless. I wondered how the lad was able to fire at all, considering his injury. Seneca rained down a flurry of blows with his huge axe, crushing at least one of the native's skulls in the process. I saw the natives throw spears at the enormous man. Two sunk into his flesh but did not seem to daunt his thirst for blood. He raised his battle axe again and swung it, catching one man so hard in the ribs that it brought him off his feet and threw him like a rag doll into three other natives who were poised to attack the big man.

On the left side I could see Omnus and Manus making light work of a few natives. They both seemed to move with such grace and elegance, striking blows with their long, curved knives that sent their enemies flailing to the ground clutching at their injuries. The two men showed no mercy to their foes, as they lay on the ground bleeding. Omnus and Manus brought their swords down upon the Ixil warriors, ending their misery with precise kill strokes.

I turned my attention to Benson, who had moved ahead of Dubois now and was reloading his shotgun. He was oblivious to the three natives behind him as they quickly got up from the ground and threw their spears at Benson's back. I watched in horror as two of the spear heads actually appeared like bright red thorns through his belly. He looked down at them in astonishment. Slowly falling to his knees, he toppled the rest of the way to the ground. Kibal skirmished with the three Ixil warriors responsible for Benson's demise.

The battle seemed to be intensifying; there were only about fifteen Ixil warriors remaining, and they had moved into a defensive position together on the right side of the camp. The rest of our party was spread out into a half circle around them. Every so often, an Ixil warrior would throw a spear, but Mendax had picked up Benson's shotgun and he and Dubois were picking the Ixil off like shooting fish in a barrel. It was as if the Ixils had never seen this type of fire power before. Finally, one of them shouted, and they all ran headlong at us. I felt my heart stop; everything seemed to morph into slow motion. I couldn't hear anything but my own breath as I inhaled and exhaled automatically. My heartbeat became rapid; I immediately brought the flare gun up and made ready. I looked at the warriors who were approaching; they had a look of terror and determination on their faces. Dr. Toepfer was the first to fire his gun, sending one native sprawling. Another native must have spotted us, and he threw his spear off somewhere on my right side. I took aim at an enemy right ahead of me and fired. The flare flew straight and true into his stomach. It seemed to burn a hole right through his insides. He screamed and used his hands to try to remove the flare, but it had done its damage and the warrior had no choice but to drop to the ground.

Custos stepped out of hiding and stood squarely in front of me as he raised his long, curved sword. An Ixil hurled a spear at him, but he parried it by swinging his sword in an arc-like motion to his right and stepping quickly to his left. He then struck the warrior across his middle. The warrior stood still as his intestines began to spill from him. They spilled out upon the jungle floor and he tried to grab at them to put them back, so to speak, into his belly area. Custos moved on to the next warrior who he slashed right across the neck, almost cleanly decapitating him. By this time the two other attacking parties had realigned themselves and were pushing hard at the Ixil warrior's backsides. We had them trapped. I saw the boy rush forward as if possessed, and try to take on a huge warrior, who stood amongst the eight remaining fighters. The boy had nothing but an arrow in his hand as he attacked with a look of pure hatred on his face. He stabbed violently with the head of the arrow, but he missed the native who quickly brought his fist down across the boy's face, knocking him to the jungle floor. I felt compelled to move suddenly, my body taking over almost instinctively before my mind could stop me. I clumsily took another flare from my pocket and loaded the gun as I moved. I somehow got the cartridge into the gun and snapped the magazine back into place. I cocked and raised the gun to aim as I moved, but I tripped over a root as I began to run and the quick jerking motion of my body caused me to fire wide of my mark. The warrior as well noticed and turned his attention towards me. I could see he had gotten out a small ax that he was going to use on the boy, but instead he turned and came toward me with a look of pure fury upon his brown face. He raised the ax as he ran towards me. I ripped out my machete and tried to regain my balance. This was the moment I had feared the night before. I seemed to sense this was the moment of my doom. I gripped the machete with two hands and waited for the Ixil to make the first move. He tried to bring the ax down on my head, but I thrust the machete up diagonally and blocked the kill thrust. I then brought the machete back across my body in a slashing motion, grazing the warrior on the chest. The blow was enough to send him back for a second. When he attacked again however, it was even more furious then the first blow. He brought the ax up in a sideways motion, and I barely got out of the way as it whooshed past my right arm. I didn't see his left fist as he brought it up swinging and catching me in the temple. There was a white light followed by stars as I fell backwards off my feet. When the stars cleared, I saw him standing over me, his ax was raised to kill me. But as he went to bring the ax down a shiny object appeared through his ribs. At first it was small, but it began to grow longer until it stuck out about six inches. Then it disappeared and the warrior fell dead. There stood Custos with his long sword, bright red and dripping the blood of the enemy.

The battle was over, and I had survived. I took a look at the carnage. All the Ixil warriors had been killed, but we had our losses too. Benson was dead, and I found out that the spear that was hurled into the jungle where we were hiding had pinned Ikal to a tree, and he had bled out. Seneca was hemorrhaging from about four massive holes in his body. He was beginning to lumber about from the loss of blood. Dr. Toepfer was beginning to heat up a knife to cauterize Seneca's wounds. Dubois had a pretty bad gash on his left arm, and Kibal had been stabbed in the foot by a spear. Other than that, the rest of the group appeared pretty much unscathed.

Seneca had already begun to scalp the Ixil warriors. The doctor had tried to get the big native to sit still so he could work on getting those wounds mended, but the brute just brushed him off. The doctor was forced to follow him around with the hot knife trying to cauterize the wounds all the while being swatted at, like a mosquito, by the big warrior. I went over to Mr. Benson's body, where he lay on his side. There was a pool of blood on his chest, and his face had a look of shocked confusion mixed with pain. I began to use my machete to dig a hole. Custos and Mendax came over to help me. We dug the hole about four feet deep and before putting Benson's body in, I emptied his pockets. He had a gold pocket watch, a picture of a woman I presumed to be his wife, and his billfold, which had the remaining money from his stipend in it. I thought it would be nice to return these articles to his widow. Kibal performed a small service over his fellow native's body, but I did not detect any real sadness on his face, I assumed it was because Ikal had died in battle and thus he had a heroic death. We gathered in the clearing as the sun sent its first rays down upon our sweating bodies. Dubois said the best plan of action was to move on as quickly as we could, for he had no clue how long it would take our haggard party to make it to the old, abandoned village. A sort of stretcher was made for Seneca who was now growing pale from blood loss. He gripped the scalps of the enemies he had killed tightly in his fist as he began to shake with fever. It took three men to carry the big native on the stretcher.

The boy led the group as we advanced, followed by Kibal then Manus, Omnus and Mendax with the stretcher. Dr. Toepfer followed behind the stretcher. I was next followed by Dubois and Custos, who brought up the rear. We made our way slowly until we were able to find another hunting trail. No one really talked much the rest of that day. I think for the most part we were all reflecting on the early morning skirmish. I thought to myself how lucky I was to be alive. The angry and bloodthirsty looks on the faces of those Ixil Warriors flashed through my memory from time to time throughout the day's hike. I knew that those faces would haunt my dreams for years to come.

It was nearly sundown when we hobbled out into a clearing. We had made it to the abandoned village. Out of one of the huts came the rest of our party. Abbitt stood looking at us with sorrow in his eyes. Grant just gaped; his mouth hung wide open in disbelief. Procul and Fortis both looked unfazed by what they saw (come to think of it, Pista's followers rarely showed much emotion). Then I saw her. The last one out of the tent. Ms. Peranio's eyes seemed to be searching as she brought her hand to her mouth as if in disbelief. Then she saw me and ran over and put her arms around me, wrapping me in the tightest hug I believe I had ever received. "Lord be praised," I heard her whisper under her breath. I put my arms around her and all of the stress and adrenaline passed from my body in that moment. I felt my body go limp in her arms. She helped me over to a spot on the ground, and she sat me down. The next thing I remember it was completely dark, and Ms. Peranio was looking me over for any injuries I might have sustained. When she did not find anything, she sat next to me then and I could feel her staring at me. All I could do was stare into the fire as it blazed in front of me.

147

The doctor came over at some point and gave me a bit of a chocolate bar. I chewed it but I couldn't taste it. Any food I would have eaten that night would have turned to ash in my mouth. Something seemed to stir within me, and I lay down on the grass and began to weep. I could feel the soft hand of Ms. Peranio on my back. Although it felt very comforting, I could not stop crying. My sides heaved with every sob, and I felt like a small child that could not be soothed. Finally, I could not even sob anymore. A haze came over me, and I closed my eyes.

Brighton Bay Sanitarium
Assistant Warden Achiel Caldwell's Log
April 28, 1949

I awoke very late the next morning. I don't think I had moved a muscle all night. I sat up and felt very stiff and sore. Ms. Peranio was the first to greet me. She took a look at my face and said, "Your back, how do you feel this morning?" I looked at her inquisitively. "What do you mean by that?" She told me I had been in shock the night before when I had arrived at the camp. Ms. Peranio had tried desperately to pull me out of my stupor, but to no avail. I had fallen asleep, and it seemed my rest had brought me out of it. It was at this moment I remembered the rest of the people in my party.
    "How is everyone else? did anyone else die during the night?" Ms. Peranio assured me everyone was fine but

148

that Seneca was suffering from a high fever. "We have sent the boy ahead to meet with his tribe and bring back help. The doctor and I both think the risk is too great in moving Seneca right now. He would most likely die on the trip." She looked a bit haggard, her hair was disheveled and her face had dried blood and dirt smeared on it. The sun's rays still bounced off her eyes, revealing that glimmer of radiance and beauty that drew me so fiercely.

As I walked through the rest of the camp and took a look at the rest of our party, I could tell that some of our company did not like the decision that was made to let the boy go. I thought about the boy. What if he came back with warriors to destroy us in order to collect more trophies? What if the boy was unable to convince his tribal leaders that we were allies and not enemies? Needless to say, I think we all felt a bit on edge the remainder of that day. It was nearing evening when an old native man stepped out from the jungle into our clearing. He wore a cape that looked like it was made from the pelt of a jaguar. Upon his wrinkled head, he wore a great hat that had various kinds of feathers protruding from it in different directions. Behind the old man stood the boy. Mr. Dubois and Kibal approached the old man and the three of them changed pleasantries in a strange language. Then Dubois turned to the rest of the group and told us to pack our things. We were to journey with the chief and some of his warriors to the Q'eqchi village. "But what about Seneca? You know we can't move him." Dubois explained that the party of natives had brought their medicine man along with them in order to treat Seneca. Doctor Toepfer did not like the idea of Seneca being alone with the Q'eqchi tribesman. The doctor wished to stay with his patient. Dubois seemed against leaving the doctor in the middle of the jungle with a bunch of natives, until Manus spoke up and said he would stay with the doctor for protection.

The rest of the group then followed the Chieftain and his warriors into the jungle toward the Q'eqchi village. A driving rain beat down on us through the canopy as we traveled long into the night. The Q'eqchi warriors had brought torches that lit our path as we trudged along. It was about 2:00 a.m. (by my watch) when we arrived at the village. We were met by the native women, who all came out of their huts and began to shriek and throw their arms up in the air above their bare breasts. They touched us as we walked by. It was a strange ritual, but Dubois assured us it was just a normal greeting. We found out later that the tribe was elated because the boy we had brought back was the chief's grandson. We were shown to some huts made of straw and we went in and collapsed from exhaustion. Little did we know that our hike had been ten miles. I was still recovering from the battle the day before, so I slept well again.

Brighton Bay Sanitarium
Assistant Warden Achiel Caldwell's Log
April 29, 1949

I awoke the following morning more refreshed than I had felt in a long time. I got up and went out to have a better look at the village. The hut our group had stayed in was set up on a little hill overlooking the rest of the village. I saw a large number of the straw huts sprawling off into the distance in no real order or pattern. This was quite some village, although for the number of huts, there were not that many natives walking about. There were the occasional groups of little children running around as children do and whispering to one another as they stared at us with their big, brown eyes. I found Ms. Peranio standing and talking to Dubois, who seemed to be pointing off into the distance. She came running over when she saw me.

"I have a surprise for you," she said as she took my hand and led me into the jungle beyond the village. It was very hot and muggy in the jungle. The storms from the night prior had left a dense humidity in the air. We wound our way down a sloping path that seemed to weave in and out through the immense trees. Their bases had to be as big around as an elephant's body, I had to crane my neck upward in order to see their foliage. When the path became level again we stumbled upon a pristine pool. Water spilled over a precipice about forty feet over our heads. The water then careened its way down through a jumble of jagged rocks, splashing into the pool below. The place seemed to be magical, like something out of a dream. The water was so clear you could see the tiny minnows swimming among the rocks at the bottom of the pool. It had to be about twenty feet deep in the middle. I had been so entranced by the scenery that I had forgotten Ms. Peranio was there with me.

"Well, are you coming in or what?" Her question startled me, and I turned to answer. But she had already hiked up her pants and was wading into the water. I hiked mine up as well and followed her in. The water felt very cool on my legs and feet. It was then I realized that my toe had not hurt since before the battle; the salve had worked very quickly to heal my little extremity! The cool water seemed to soak into my feet, allowing all the sweat and the dirt to slowly be rinsed into the pool.

"Feels good, doesn't it." Mattie said. "

It feels great, thank you for bringing me here." I was actually surprised at how relaxed I was becoming.

"I thought you were the perfect person to share this with."

I was a bit tongue-tied. "Well, thank you for thinking of me."

"I've been thinking about you a lot lately, ever since you said you volunteered to fight the Ixil. That night, I couldn't sleep; I was worrying about your safety. I couldn't understand why. Then the next day as we traveled, I felt something that I have never felt before. I feared it was too late, and I feared I would never have a moment like this to share with you."

We waded around the outer bank headed for the waterfall. It seemed Mattie wanted to get close and personal with the running water. We were almost there when I saw Mattie slip and fall into the water. I quickly ran to her side and tried to pull her from the water, but her weight and my bad footing caused me to fall down as well. I was fully submerged. The water was very cold, and it took my body a second to adjust. Then I stood up out of the water. I turned to look at Ms. Peranio. She was still sitting in the water with her head thrown back laughing hysterically. I started to laugh too as I sat down beside her. The water now felt very soothing, as if my body was cleansing itself of all the hard work and sweat that had built up over the past couple of days.

Mattie looked at me now with her eyes glowing strangely. I reached over and removed a few strands of hair that had fallen into her eyes. As I did it seemed as if she started to lean towards me. My brain started to alert me to the strangeness of the situation, but my body started to act as if it were on a different circuit. I could feel myself leaning in too. Suddenly, a noise from somewhere near the pool caused us both to stop what we were doing and look up. It was a small group of Q'eqchi children running toward the pool in order to swim. I looked back at Mattie, and I could see the glow in her eyes. It was as vibrant and clear as I had ever seen. Yet her expression was one of subtle yearning. "We best be getting back to the village; we don't want anyone missing us. I also think we should keep this quiet. I don't want anyone thinking I'm off doing... things. People might get the wrong impression; you understand," I said almost dutifully. Mattie's expression changed immediately, and I could see that she felt hurt.

"I'm sorry," I said as we wadedd back to the edge of the pool to get out. She did not answer me but shoved her socks and boots back on and stormed back to the village. I followed behind her, and when I got back to the village I saw that I wasn't too far off from my statement. Dubois immediately approached me, "We need to have a meeting immediately in order to figure out a plan for continuing into the jungle and finding the lost city."

I followed him back to one of the huts on the hill, but I couldn't get my mind off of Ms. Peranio. I had kissed her! That was the first kiss I had ever received from a woman. I had to push the memory from my mind as I entered the hut. Grant sat with Custos and Mendax on one side of the hut.   Abbitt, Kibal and the Chieftain of the Q'eqchi village sat on the other side. I sat next to Custos, while Dubois sat next to Kibal. We were without our main translator, Seneca, so this whole process was going to be more difficult. Seneca was our main go-between in most conversations between natives and English-speaking people.   Luckily, Dubois was able to understand most of the Spanish dialect that Kibal spoke. Kibal could take Seneca's place. The conversation started rather abruptly.

"We need to ask the chieftain for help in finding this lost city of Kul. Kibal, ask the chief if he knows where the city might be located."

"What did he say?" Grant wanted to know.

"The chief has heard of this place," Dubois responded, "and has an idea of where it might be. But he says that is wild land. Not even the natives wander into that part of the jungle."

"Why is it that they don't go to find the city?" Abbitt asked.

"The chief says it has been long known by all the tribes that this area is forbidden. He says it is guarded by monsters."

"Pshh... Old wives' tales if you ask me."

Dubois was quick to add, "The Q'eqchi are a very superstitious people. They have seen things in this jungle that the rest of civilization have never witnessed. It would be good to keep that in mind before brushing this warning off like you have, Mr. Grant."

"What if the chief led us to the edge of his kingdom and then drew us a map in order to get us to where he thinks the city of Kul may be," queried Custos.

Kibal asked the chief our question. The elderly man sat quietly for some time, obviously lost in thought. Then he shook his head up and down. He began to draw a picture in the dirt floor of the hut. He was obviously showing Kibal where he thought the city might be. Abbitt took out a pen and notebook and started to draw the map for reference. Kibal finally relayed the information to Dubois, who then turned and addressed us.

"The Chieftain will send his best warriors to lead us to the edge of his lands. From there, we must follow this map. He says that there are four big boulders in the jungle that look like heads in a sort of line. If we can find all four heads/boulders, we will be close to the city."

Abbitt chimed in, "Did he say how long the trip might take?"

 The chief seems to think that the city is only two days' journey into the unknown. Of course, he's only speculating," responded Dubois.

 "When do we leave?" Custos asked.

"The natives would like to throw a ceremony for us tonight to thank us for bringing back their young chieftain," Dubois explained.

I was dumbfounded. "Wait, the boy is royalty?"

"Yes, this man here is the boy's grandfather. He says that the boy's father died in battle."

I instantly felt awful for the boy, losing his own father at such a young age. The meeting seemed to end on the sad news as if everyone was suddenly so filled with remorse that they could not speak. One by one we started to file out of the hut. I was one of the last to leave, and as I came out into the sun I could see that a large group of natives had gathered. I thought it somewhat strange. Then I felt a wet hand grab my arm. I looked down; it was the boy we had saved. He was kneeling on the ground with his head bowed looking at the dirt. He called out a few phrases that sounded like gibberish to my untrained ears. Then he let go of my arm and fell face down in front of me and attempted to kiss my shoe. I backed away, somewhat unnerved by the situation. Then I looked at my arm. The boy's hand had been wet with blood. The sticky red droplets formed the shape of a hand. I looked at Dubois for some sort of answer to this madness. Dubois turned to Kibal, who answered in a somewhat shocked manner. Dubois furrowed his brow as he translated, "The boy is pledging his life to you. He will be your servant and never leave your side."

My mouth dropped open in utter disbelief. "What? Why would he want to serve me? He will be a chief one day. How do I tell him I don't want this?" Dubois looked at me with a bit of anger in his eyes, "You cannot tell him that. He has already pledged himself to you in front of witnesses. If you told him you don't want him, he will be forced to end his own life right here and now."

I took another look at the boy. Just then the chief came over and looked at the boy with sad eyes. He said something to the boy who was crouching motionless on the ground. Then the old man went over to a pile of wet earth and picked it up in his hands. He spat in the mud and then spoke to his people. With tears rolling down his wrinkled cheeks, he smeared mud on the boy's head.

"What just happened?" I asked somewhat under my breath. The natives slowly turned and headed back to their huts in complete silence. The chief walked off as well, his shoulders drooped and his head hanging as he entered his hut.

When they were gone Dubois spoke: "The chief just disowned the boy. It was necessary for the boy to be disowned in order for him to be your servant. The chief could have seen fit to kill the boy instead."

I was confused and I couldn't seem to wrap my mind around what was happening. *Why was this happening to us – to me?* Dubois spoke again, "The chief will keep his word. We will leave tomorrow, so I suggest we rest up."

We all went our separate ways. When I turned to go to my hut the boy rose and began to follow me. Needless to say there was no ceremony that night; no celebration for the return of their future leader. He had changed all of that; he would rather serve me than lead a tribe and be treated like a king. I pondered on that for the rest of the night until I fell asleep.

The Legends of Green Eagle
Interpreted by: Benito Cajero
Told by: Ta'awa Hotsko
Calabre X

Dominebris called upon Tangella the mother of the Strix. She flew him away to live in the clouds with the Strix for some time. Dominebris left the Soparli in charge of the human cities. Tapani became ruler over the cities of men. He did not treat the humans well, but instead asked for sacrifices from them. When the people could not offer goods, they had to resort to human sacrifices. Tangella had one of her Strix spies watch Tapani and his actions. She reported back about what Tapani was doing. Dominebris sent a Strix messenger to Tapani whose name was Lien. "Dominebris has decreed that you will be punished if you do not stop your awful treatment of the children of the Incendit." Tapani was enraged by this, and he had his guards throw Lien in prison. A moon passed and then Dominebris, along with Tangella and many of the Strix sisters came to Tapani. Dominebris wanted answers. "Where is Lien, and why have you not listened to my warning?" Tapani answered, "I did not think it necessary to listen to you when you gave me control over the human cities. As for your precious messenger, you may have her back." He gestured to his guards and they brought in Lien's head on a spike and presented it to Tangella. Dominebris was furious. "You have ruined the relations of my kin. I shall go and deliberate your fate." Upon making that brief statement, he turned to leave and the days that followed were filled with rumors of war between the great beasts.

Brighton Bay Sanitarium
Assistant Warden Achiel Caldwell's Log
April 30, 1949

We had to be up and ready to go early the next morning. Our smaller party met by the edge of the village; two Q'eqchi warriors waited for us. Once again, our party began to journey deeper into the Yucatan wilderness. We were able to keep on trails for most of the day, but later in the afternoon rains began to fall again, drenching the entire party. When it began to get dark the two warriors leading the party stopped, and Dubois told us to set up camp.

The warriors then took Dubois, Abbitt, Kibal Custos and me ahead about a mile. The trail we had been following ended abruptly and the natives halted. They both pointed their fingers in the direction of the gloomy rainforest in front of us. The message was relayed to Dubois, who then told us that this was the end of the Q'eqchi land. He went on to say that the first boulder would be a short distance into the foliage. We then went back to the camp and the two Q'eqchi warriors quickly said their goodbyes and scampered back to their own village like rabbits running from a fox. They were obviously quite apprehensive about this territory! I think some of us were focusing on what the chief had said, "Monsters control the forbidden part of the forest." Would we run into these monsters on our travels?

We set up a night watch system, and Dubois said if it rained in the morning we might as well try to wait it out. I had the last night watch. Having had the early morning hours with Custos again, I awoke and emerged from my tent. There was an oil lamp lit and placed at the center of the camp. Lightning and thunder broke the still, dark silence of the sleeping jungle. The rain had only intensified during the night. It had been storming for the last four or five hours. With my new shadow, I walked over and we sat on a log across from Custos. We sat in silence for some time, but then Custos began to speak to me.

"What is it we are doing here, Achiel?"

"I don't exactly know what you mean by that, Custos," I replied.

"I mean, what did we come all this way to do? Are you still chasing a deranged killer? Or has this trip never been about Patronis? Perhaps you are looking for something else?"

"Did you talk to Pista before we left?" I asked frankly. I see he told you about our conversation. I can't lie to you, Custos. What Mr. Pista said has been weighing very heavily on my mind. I'm beginning to believe that Patronis might not be as insane as everyone thinks he is. The more I witness things on this trip, I'm beginning to believe that he is after something very important."

"Yes, but what makes this "thing" that Patronis searches for so special, Achiel? Why would he come to the middle of a jungle in order to find this "thing'? What is he going to do if he finds it?"

It was time to level with him. "Custos, do you believe in the 'Fountain of Youth?'"

"I don't have to believe in anything. All I was asked to do was to watch over you and make sure nothing happens to you. You must search your heart to find the answers. You must do what is necessary to bring an end to all of this."

I didn't know how to answer him. None of what he said made any sense to me. I looked over at the boy, who stared deeply into the gas lamp as if transfixed by its glow. Custos must have seen me, because he changed the subject.

"The boy is very brave to give up what he had in order to come with you."

"I still can't figure out what made him decide that; I mean he can't even communicate with me. How is he supposed to serve me?"

"He heard of your bravery during the fighting. Kibal told him of how you came to his rescue before that warrior could kill him. He thought that you showed great power and might in your actions; thus, he wanted to be your servant in order to learn how to be brave, how to become a true warrior so to speak."

"I didn't even kill the warrior who attacked him. That was you! And besides, Ms. Peranio took the arrow out of his shoulder. Isn't that considered 'saving his life' too?"

"He senses something in you. Only true warriors have a certain glow; it is as much a sense as smelling or tasting, but it is only given to certain individuals. The boy thinks you possess that warrior sense."

I began to insist. "I'm not a warrior! I'm not brave! I fell apart after that battle. Ms. Peranio said I had a nervous breakdown at the abandoned village the night after the battle."

"Achiel, bravery is not determined by how one lives his life but rather by what they do under dire circumstances." Custos's voice was almost tender. "It is when a person is under fire that his true self is revealed. Never forget that."

I was finished speaking to Custos. He obviously thought too highly of me, and I could not grasp why that was. I just knew at some point I would let him down and that thought gave me great anxiety. I looked at the boy; he sat next to me looking around into the darkness. A few days ago he would never have sat so close to Custos. I noticed how the lad's attitude had changed toward the big dark fellow. *He must be getting used to the man,* I thought to myself. We sat quietly for the rest of the watch. I went back to my tent completely drenched and in a foul mood after my conversation with Custos. I fell asleep rather quickly, but not as quickly as the boy lying behind me, his light snoring making me even angrier.

Brighton Bay Sanitarium
Assistant Warden Achiel Caldwell's Log
May 1, 1949

I awoke late in the morning. It was still raining heavily when I got up and ate some dried fruit. It reminded me of my time at Natavis, where the sun shone bright and warm upon the dry desert climate. I didn't think I would ever dry out from my time in the rainforest. I felt like a sponge so full of water that it could not hold any more. The wet seemed to be reaching my bones, and I was always waking up shivering. The rain seemed to zap me of any energy I might have possessed otherwise. I just lay awake in my tent listening to the soft plunks of rain splashing against my tent. I laid there for what seemed like hours, but the rain never let up.

Finally, around 11:00 o'clock someone spoke to me from outside my tent; it was Dubois.

"We will be moving in an hour. You might want to start packing up, Dr. Caldwell." I got up slowly and began to pack. I felt my movements seemed like those of a sloth. The boy helped me put my things in my pack. He seemed to be in a jovial mood. I figured I may as well start trying to communicate with him (especially if he was going to be my shadow for the rest of my existence). So I got his attention, pointed at myself and said, "Achiel." He looked at me with no expression and then went back to his work. I must have tried at least four or five more times, doing the same thing each time and getting no response from the boy at all. Around noon we left our camp and moved into the thick jungle. Dubois and Kibal used machetes to blaze a path for the rest of the group.

It was around two o'clock in the afternoon when we came to the first boulder. It stood at least fifteen feet high and twenty feet wide. The boulder seemed to have two large indents up near the top that looked like eye sockets. To one side of the large rock was a drawing of what looked like two figures with crossed spears. Dubois took it to be a sign that we were headed in the right direction, so we continued. Around seven in the evening, as the gloom of the night overtook the grey of the day, we happened upon the second boulder. This one was more hidden by vines and shrubs, but as we hacked away at them we found that a great hole had been bored into the base of the boulder. With the limited amount of light left in the jungle the boulder looked like a screaming skull. We set up camp under the protection of the large boulder. We were able to get a fire going, and we all sat around it for some time trying to dry out our clothing and bodies. Our teeth began to chatter; it seemed as if this part of the jungle was colder than the rest of the rainforest at night. Even Custos and the other workers looked somewhat paler than normal. Everyone put their socks and boots on sticks and hung them as close to the fire as they dared.

The rain continued long into the night, and I don't believe anybody kept watch. The rain had zapped all of our energy. No one woke me at four in the morning to take my watch either.

Brighton Bay Sanitarium
Assistant Warden Achiel Caldwell's Log
May 2, 1949

Around six this morning I lifted my head to look around. It was still somewhat dark, although the darkness was starting to take certain forms. The fire had gone out and the rain had stopped sometime during the night. I sat up and listened. The jungle was eerily quiet, unnervingly so. There had always been noise while we trudged through the jungle: sounds of animals moving, birds flapping or crying to one another, trees swaying or stirring. But now that the rain had stopped not a single sound broke the silence.

I crawled over to the fire and tried to find an ember to rekindle a flame. I did so slowly and soon the fire was warming me once more. The other members of the party ambled over to sit by the fire. Ms. Peranio chose her seat directly across from me and next to Grant. She had not even looked at me since our little rendezvous at the Q'eqchi village. I had been so preoccupied by our journey I had not noticed until now. I began to wonder if I had done something wrong to receive this treatment. I thought that what I had said to her made me look strong. I was trying to impress her with my dedication to this journey and show her that I was serious about my job as leader. Maybe she took my statements to mean something else. It made my stomach sick just thinking about it. I thought the world of Ms. Peranio and didn't want what I said to be the end of any sort of relationship that we might have had. I purposed in my heart to try to talk to her soon.

We ate dried meat of some sort that the Q'eqchi had given us for our travels. It was enough to warm up my wet cold stomach. We began to pack up at about eight o'clock. Walking around to the side of the big boulder, we found the same inscription we had seen on the first head. We then made our way through the thick wet jungle in a straight line from the last rock. There was a cool fog that hung in the jungle; it blanketed the tops of the trees from view. Every once in a while a swirl of fog could be seen like cotton hanging on a shrub or vine that was close to the ground. At about midday we stopped, and Dubois began to deliberate with Abbitt. The talk was about how we should have seen the third boulder by now.

All of a sudden a cool wind began to blow through the canopy in a downward direction, bringing the high hanging fog down upon us like a blanket. I could not even see Custos who stood not three feet in front of me. Dubois called out over the wind for us to take each other's' hands. I grabbed Custos's hand and then grabbed the boy, who was standing behind me. We moved like a chain forging a path that we could not even see. We moved probably a half a mile before the fog cleared and our visibility was restored.

Then Grant called out from behind me, "where is Mattie?" felt my body go cold with fear. She was not with the group. We all turned back immediately and made our way through what was left of the fog, all the while calling for Ms. Peranio. About ten minutes later we heard screams coming from our right. I knew it was her by the sound of the voice, and I dashed into the untamed jungle like a bull on a rampage. Vines and bushes caught my clothing and barred my way, but I batted them aside and continued my half-crazed charge into the forest following the screams. A rogue vine caught my leg and I tripped, falling face first onto the wet earth. I got up and brushed myself off, but when I looked up, I saw something that made me choke on what little breath I had left.

There in front of me was a severed head on a stick. Its flesh was hanging in many places from the white bones of the skull underneath. When I had my jagged breath somewhat under control, I realized that I had stumbled upon a path and there behind me stood Ms. Peranio, white with fear. The rest of the party slowly emerged from the forest, and we regrouped by the deadly road marker. Dubois thought that this was the path we were looking for. Mattie had to be calmed down. Doctor Toepfer came and started to rub her hands and tell her all would be well. Slowly the color began to return in her cheeks, and before long she told the doctor she was ready to continue. We surmised that we must have gotten off track in the fog. We walked down the path that seemed to be an old road. It was at least two feet wide, and every fifty feet a skull on a stick marked it. The wind still blew gently, and soon we could hear what sounded like native drums in the distance. The road began to slope slightly upward as we followed the sound of the drums.

"I thought this jungle was void of any native tribes," Abbitt said, trying to reassure everyone, even himself. We got closer and closer to the beating of the drums. Dubois had us stop, and he sent Kibal ahead with Manus to scout the road. They returned an hour later and relayed that they had found the third boulder. This one had hollowed logs suspended around it from the closest trees, and when the wind blew the logs would hit the boulder, emitting the eerie drum sound. We set up camp at the third boulder. The road seemed to continue further into the jungle, but night was coming on and Dubois thought it would be better to wait until morning before traveling the rest of the way. No one got much sleep that night. The jungle was still dead quiet. I had not heard or seen an animal all day. There was something very strange about this part of the jungle. It looked like there was a major influence of mankind, what with the road and the logs and the skulls on sticks. Yet the chieftain had said this was forbidden to all indigenous tribes. We set up a watch for the night as we organized our tents around the base of the third boulder. I had exuded a lot of energy when I ran through the jungle looking for Ms. Peranio, so I slept heavily. Unfortunately, my sleep could not keep the horrible dreams away.

The Legends of Green Eagle
Interpreted by: Benito Cajero
Told by: Ta'awa Hotsko
Calabre XI

Dominebris deliberated with the Strix for many days until it was decided that the Strix would go to war with the Soparli. A message was sent via the humans to Tapani and the two forces met on the battlefield to put an end to Tapani. The war raged for many hours and both Strix and Soparli fell dead. When the fighting became very intense Dominebris ran with Tangella to try to cut down Tapani. Dominebris fought valiantly against Tapani, but in the end he was dealt a great blow. As Dominebris fell the fighting stopped and all of the Strix and Soparli rushed to their master's side. Tangella slowly lifted Dominebris's body and flew away with it. The Strix and Soparli were both stricken with great sadness and shame for what they had done. As for Dominebris, it is said that Tangella dropped his body into the ocean, never to be seen or heard from again. Quomvi Ta'aho gathered the remaining forces of the warring factions of the Semper Nefas. A tornado of lightning and blue flame was upon a hill. It spoke to the creatures,
"You have killed your own master! You have made an end of his influence, and although you have done this out of greed, you shall be rewarded, for you are now my servants to do with as I wish. For the Soparli, you will be able to cause pain to humans with a simple touch.
For the Sapator, you can change humans into your kind and likeness.

For the Syreni, you can change a human's past and control their destiny.

Finally, for the Strix, who served Dominebris until his end, you can indwell humans and live for them.

These are the gifts I bestow upon my servants, use them wisely."

With that the tornado disappeared and the Semper Nefas mourned the loss of Dominebris.

Brighton Bay Sanitarium
Assistant Warden Achiel Caldwell's Log
May 3, 1949

I dreamt that I was jogging through the jungle; the vines and bushes pulling at me from all directions, slowing my progress. Ahead of me I could hear the screams, and I desperately fought to move forward but I seemed to be getting nowhere quickly. Then from behind me I heard a deep, guttural roar that could only be that of a large monster. I looked behind me and saw the trees shake as if something large was moving through them toward me. I fought harder, still trying to move forward and racing to get away from the beast that pursued me. Finally, I heard a whispering voice call out my name. "Achiel Caldwell," it echoed in my ears. The voice seemed to be coming from above me. I looked up but could see nothing but trees. "Achiel Caldwell," it called again. Then I realized I was asleep and immediately opened my eyes to discover it was someone calling me for watch. I answered quietly, "All right, I'm coming; just a second."

I began to sit up. "Do not move!" the voice almost hissed with anger. I froze. "You did not listen to my warning, human. You are in great danger here. Even now it may be too late. You must tell your party to turn back. Nothing but death awaits you at the Temple of Kul."

It did exist then! This whole trip was not in vain, and Patronis would possibly be waiting for us. Then I thought to myself, *what if the voice I was hearing was that of Patronis*? "Patronis?" I said as I slowly reached for a lamp. There was a large whooshing sound that came from outside my tent. It woke the boy, who had been sleeping at the foot of the bedroll. I quickly opened the tent flap to examine the camp. I lifted my lamp and looked at the ground around the area, scanning the outskirts of the camp for any sign of foliage moving. There was nothing at all, so I went to look in on the watch. Grant and Kibal, were both asleep at their posts. I woke them up and told them to go to their tents. I was going to scour the area to try and find clues as to who had just warned me. I took my lamp and went around the edge of the road to look for footprints coming in or leaving the camp. I found nothing, and then I went over to my tent and examined all around it. There was one set of deep prints on the right side of my tent, as if the person had been ready to jump. I looked around the other tents but saw no other tracks. It didn't make sense. It also made me suspect that it was not Patronis. Although I was slightly relieved by that notion,

I was filled with a new dread that something else was out here watching me. I went and sat next to the boy and built up the fire again from the previous night. The orange

flames made the surrounding landscape even more frightening. Finally, after what seemed like an eternity, the grey skies lightened and everything took form.

Our party got up somewhat early because the excitement of walking down an actual road after trudging through a dense forest for so long boosted everyone's morale. We were on the road by seven in the morning, walking at a cautious pace. We came upon the fourth and final boulder at nine o'clock; it was even more terrifying than the others before it. The boulder had been carved to look like a skull. Some sort of red paint had been splattered like rivulets of blood pouring from the eye sockets. We went around to the right side of the rock, but there was no picture. Confused, we circled the boulder and found a drawing on the left side this time. It was a human head on a spike. Dubois had no idea what the picture meant. He scratched his head as he conferred with Kibal. Finally, they decided that this was a message that explained the road going south. We determined to continue on the road and it should lead us right to the city. We strapped up and continued.

We had walked about five miles when the brick road began to break apart. Plants and bushes shot up through the path, and we had to maneuver to stay on it. Dubois thought we should keep going. The bricks began to appear spaced further apart, and the path was impeded by even more brush. Still, we continued onward until there was nothing but jungle in front of us. The road completely disappeared, and the terrain began to take a steep decline. Dubois shook his head in confusion. I could see that many of the other travelers were beginning to lose hope as well. We had by this time walked more than seven miles past the fourth boulder. The whole road had been an uphill climb; we were all exhausted.

Dubois told us to eat our lunch while he deliberated with Kibal about what to do. At about mid-afternoon Dubois told us to travel back down the hill toward the fourth boulder. We would regroup there and search the surrounding terrain. It took us three hours to get back, and when we did it was decided that we would stay there for the night. We had hiked the largest number of miles since being in the jungle and so much of it uphill. My legs hurt, and all I wanted to do was lay down and sleep. The rest of the party built a fire, but I decided not to join them. I had risen very early this morning and had not slept much the night before. I needed to recuperate.

It was late that night when I sat straight up in bed. I could hear something outside. I snuck past my sleeping servant boy, trying not to make a sound. I unzipped my tent and stepped out without waking him. For the first time since entering the forbidden part of the forest, the moon was evident. The almost iridescent beams poured soft light on everything. There were even small patches of light in the jungle where the moonlight snuck in through the canopy. I took my lamp and followed the sound; it seemed to be coming from further off in the jungle. I hesitated at the edge of the road. It was not smart to go alone into the unknown, but I thought perhaps I could find out what had been spying on me. I gathered my courage and ever so carefully made my way into the jungle toward the sound. I had walked for about ten minutes when I stopped and listened. The mysterious sound came from ahead of me and I sensed it much closer now. I blew out my lamp and waited for my eyes to adjust to the darkness. I wanted to be the one to spy on whatever was out there rather than give away my position. Once my eyes were fully accustomed, I crept closer to the sound ahead of me. It seemed as if it were coming from two very different parts of the jungle. *Was there more than one creature out here?* I wondered fearfully. I got to a point where I could see something moving in front of me through the trees but could not determine what it was. I dared to get a bit closer, but as I did the creature scampered through a very dense brush and I did not hear another sound. Then suddenly from ahead of me I heard a laugh. I had heard that laugh before; I knew instantly who it was.

"Come out here, Doctor, come and behold the beauty of this place." I had to brace myself against a tree to keep from fainting. The thing I had been following was Gabriel Patronis, and he knew I was behind him. I slowly made my way out of the forest about ten feet from where he squeezed through the underbrush. He stood there with a giant smile on his face. His hair was cut short and his beard looked very haggard. He wore the remnants of what I supposed were clothes; they had been ripped to shreds by the jungle. He looked very thin, but I'm sure I had lost weight on our journey as well. He was the first to speak:

"I've travelled so long to get here, and now that I am here I feel it only right that you should be able to enjoy this moment with me. You see there, it is the Temple of Kul. There is a great treasure being concealed within the temple's cavern. It is a gift to the evil ones, a gift that has brought nothing but pain and suffering to all who have used it."

I was so grateful to finally confront my nemesis. "You have come to seek the Fountain of Youth. I know the fountain has been the subject of your search, for I know this has been your mission all along. Once you take it for yourself, what then?"

"You know of my quest and yet you still do not believe that I will find what I am looking for. Open your eyes, Doctor. You have made this journey as well. As for my mission, the Fountain of Youth is only the beginning. There is still much work to be done."

"Do you know why I have come here, Gabriel?"

"You have come to help me, to be my reinforcement." Here he hesitated. It seemed almost as though he was marshaling his own courage. "You have come to fight this impossible battle with me. You see I am tired of being alone in my 'madness' I cannot carry this burden much farther on my own, I am going to need someone who is willing to help me. Why does the world see me as crazy, when I am just trying to do the work of my creator?"

"I have been ordered by the sanitarium and a Mr. Pista to…." but I could not finish the sentence.

Patronis smiled at me kindly, "Search your heart, Doctor. You may have started this journey with those intentions, but there is a change that has come over you; I can sense it.

Deep down I knew that something was off in this whole case. Patronis began to walk closer to me; his eyes had a gentle look in them. The bags that used to hang under his eyes like clam shells had all but disappeared. His face was not that of an insane person, but rather someone who felt compassion for my situation. It was as if Patronis could see through me to my spirit. As he crept closer I instinctively wanted to back away, but my body would not respond. I felt stuck as he came ever closer.

"Will you share my burden? Will you carry part of this load?" Patronis's question was heartfelt. "It is a choice that you must make for yourself. I can sense goodness in you; I believe that you are willing to do the right thing in every situation. That is a quality that only true leaders possess."

Patronis was now about three feet from me. He raised his hand palm up towards me, almost as if he were asking me to dance. I felt something deep within me; a tiny voice spoke in a whisper, *"Trust him."* I stood there for what seemed like several lifetimes, wondering whether I should rely on the voice or just run away. Finally, the small voice had become a shrill screaming that shook my insides, and I grabbed his hand with force.

I heard him whisper, "To the end of time."

Brighton Bay Sanitarium
Assistant Warden Achiel Caldwell's Log
May 4, 1949

When I awoke I was laying in the woods, my body felt somewhat tingly. I shook off the cobwebs and tried to remember what had just happened. It was bright, and the grey sky looked ready to burst with rain. I stood up and looked around. I was still very close to the city of Kul. I ran out of the jungle and looked at the temple for the first time. It was built with enormous grey stones and it towered over most of the forest. I remembered the night before when I had been talking to Patronis. I had been careful never to take my eyes off him. Where had he gone and how far was I away from the rest of my party? I began to yell their names, waiting for any response. At first no sound came to my ears, but then slowly I began to hear voices far off. We called to one another for the next half hour until finally they appeared through the jungle. They came running out of the dense foliage. Abbitt was in awe of the temple. While Custos clapped me on the back, Dubois told me he was worried that natives had stolen me away. I told them all how I had seen Patronis the night before and that he had knocked me out and evaded me. We all split up to look for any signs of where he might have gone.

Mendax called us all over to the back side of the Temple. There was an inscription on it. Abbitt took a close look and determined that the inside of the temple was actually an old tomb for the ancient rulers of the Mayans. Dubois thought that Patronis probably went inside to look for his prize. We all agreed and went around to the front of the temple and climbed the steep, narrow steps leading to the top of the large structure. At the top was the most beautiful view of the rainforest one could hope to get. As I stood and looked out over what appeared to be an eternity of jungle, the rain began to fall, and off to the east ominous storm clouds were gathering, like warriors readying for battle. Lightning streaked across the sky and the distant soft rumble of thunder gave us a new anxiety of what was soon to come crashing down upon our heads. Luckily the temple had a roof-like structure, and the floors were sunken into the inside of the structure to keep its inhabitants out of the elements. We all wandered around looking for some sort of door that would allow entry into the tombs within.

Abbitt was the first to spot a large rock that had a metal handle. It took two of our men to remove it, and when we did we saw a staircase leading down. We slowly and cautiously descended the stairs, lighting our lamps as we went. The inside had a maze of corridors and sets of stairs leading ever downward. There were rooms that seemed to be walled off within the passages. Abbitt assumed that these were the actual tombs themselves. Once or twice he stopped near one of the rooms, looking longingly at the brick walls. It was like he was a little boy on

Christmas Day and there in front of him was a large package, but he was not allowed to look inside. We continued downward, weaving back and forth. We had gone past ten floors, each of which housed a large tomb at the bottom level. The hall turned to the left and then ended abruptly.

"This can't be right! There must be a separate room that houses the treasure. They would not put something that is supposed to give life in a tomb," Abbitt reasoned. He held his lantern up to look at the far wall where there was an inscription. It was a picture of the inside of the temple, but there was one part that did not make sense. At the bottom of the temple was a hallway that seemed to drop straight down. Abbitt felt all over the stone wall. "It's a door, and this passage lies beyond it. Help me push." With the help of three others the huge rock wall began to slide upward, and there behind the door was a tiny room with a gaping hole in the floor. We all looked at each other questioningly. Dubois took out his flare gun and shot a flare into the hole to see how far it went, but the flare disappeared completely from view. This was obviously some sort of large cavern. We deliberated on what to do. Some thought we should tie our ropes together to see if we couldn't make one gigantic rope and lower someone down. We decided that no matter how we tied the ropes together, they would never support anyone's weight.

The deliberating had taken a good amount of time, so some of our party began to sit next to the ground. We all finally fell silent. We were stumped. Our journey had brought us this far and yet, even though we were so close, it felt as though we were as distant from our goal as when we started. I was almost positive Patronis had found a way down into the cavern. When it had been quiet for some time, Procul got up and went to the edge of the hole. He turned his head as if listening to something inside the cavern.

"Do any of you hear that?" he asked us. We all shook our heads no, and then he raised himself to his feet and shook the dust from his hand and knees. "I want to try something," he said and then instantly jumped into the pit. We all let out a collective gasp and crowded around the rim of the hole to try to get a glimpse of the falling man. No such hope

"Was he mad?" Abbitt asked Custos. Custos simply raised his shoulders in a gesture of cluelessness. Then from very deep somewhere a tiny voice reached our ears. It was faint but it was Procul.

"It's all right. I'm fine; all you have to do is jump."

We couldn't believe our ears! It was definitely Procul's voice though. "I'm going," announced Omnus, and suddenly he was gone. We waited again and now two voices were heard from somewhere below us. Everyone was still hesitant, but Dubois was the next to jump and

183

then Mendax and Kibal followed. Custos took one look at me, and he could see that I was deathly afraid. Before I could stop him, he grabbed me and we both fell into the pit. I was still wrapped in Custos's arms, but I could feel wind rushing past us as we fell head first into the pit. We seemed to fall forever, but suddenly I could feel wind from what seemed to be many directions hitting us and slowing us down. The wind began to be stronger and much warmer the farther we fell. Custos pulled up on our bodies so that now we were in a parallel position. He told me to spread my legs and arms. I did as I was told, and we began to slow even more. I started to feel warm water droplets on my hands. They became more prevalent, almost like rain. Then a pocket of strong air hit me in the face. I gagged a bit. Another pocket of air hit us, and this time it was as if the strong air almost stopped our descent then without warning we hit deep water. Custos waited until we had settled in the water and then we swam to the surface. There to our right were remnants of our party on a beach that was lit up by a weird yellow glow. We swam over to them and waited for the rest of our party to jump. The boy was the next to come hurtling down; he was probably chasing me. The only people left were Grant, Ms. Peranio and Abbitt. Then we heard a scream that seemed to be coming to a crescendo with every passing second. Before long, Grant, Abbitt and Ms. Peranio came plopping into the water together. They swam over to us and we helped them onto the beach.

There ahead of us was a cave. Unfortunately, we had left all of our gear up in the temple, so if we found any more obstacles we would probably not be able to overcome them. I only had my little green book and my necklace left. We walked for about an hour in the cave. I found out that the strange flow came from a certain worm that lived within the cave. They coated the walls of the long passageway we walked along. The air was very hot due to being so far within the earth and the heat that the geyser produced. The cave slowly descended even more, becoming tighter and tighter, until finally we had to get on our hands and knees. The cave came to a halt, other than a tiny crawl space only big enough for one person at a time. Procul offered to go first again, and he began to shimmy his way into the crawl space. We all anxiously waited for him. Then he called to us from the other side that it was safe for us to come on through, because it was merely another room. We all took turns crawling through until we were all inside a large area on the other side. In the middle of the room was a platform with nothing on it. I instantly figured out what had happened. Patronis had come down here the night before, after he had knocked me unconscious.

From the other side of the room came a voice. "Looking for something?" It was not Patronis. I had never heard this voice before. "Custos, I should have known you would be mixed up in this rabble." This was obviously someone who knew something about Pista's guardsman, but how? And what was this person doing all the way out here?

"We've come to take Patronis back with us, Jian." Custos was all business and seemed to have forgotten us.

"You are too late," Jian responded, "We have captured him and are taking him to Tangella. She will know how to pass judgment on him. As for all of you, the High Council has agreed we shall kill you all, here below ground where no one will ever find you."

This Jian must have been standing in the shadows, because I could not see him or whether he had anyone with him. There were no bugs in this room; only the middle of the room had some sort of artificial light to it. But it showed straight down at the ground like a single ray from the sun. The outskirts of the room were covered in a blanket of darkness.

"You forget, Jian, we are the soldiers. You are nothing more than a slave who digs the dirt to kill time during your miserable existence!"

"You will lose your tongue for that insult, and I will personally cut it from your mouth." Jian retorted. With that, Jian and a hoard of large-bodied men came charging at us from across the room like fiends. Mendax, Procul, Custos and Omnus got in front of the rest of the party, and pulled their curved swords out and began to slice away at the charging men. The light from the blades seemed much dimmer now than it had been the last time I had seen them. The rest of us backed against the wall, instantly realizing we had no weapons. Mendax took on two chargers and immediately cut them down. Custos chopped the hand off of another. The hand flew in our direction, and it was holding a sort of metal spike. Dubois saw an opportunity and grabbed the weapon. He then advanced on the enemy parrying and cutting through the air against one of the attackers. He finally put the spike through the man's neck, dropping him instantly. Mendax, Procul, Custos and Omnus were methodically working their way forward.

"Follow us! There is a way out up here." I grabbed one of the spikes off of the dead enemy and threw the other to Grant. We both joined in the fray, taking on any of the enemy who made it through our front line. Every once in a while, a spike would come whistling past our defenses, one of them landing in the far wall and catching Abbitt square in the throat. Ms. Peranio screamed with fright. Kibal moved to grab the spike, and he came forward to join the group. We had moved forward enough that we could see the door on the far side. It was our only chance. By now some of the enemy had flanked us and we were encircled. Dubois got caught on the outside of the circle and was immediately pounced on by four attackers. I could not see as they surrounded him as they had melted off behind the other attackers. Dubois was gone!

We finally made it to the door and advanced out into a long hallway that started to slope upwards. Custos and Omnus took the forward position, while Mendax and Procul took the covered the back. In the midst of them Ms. Peranio, Kibal, Grant, the boy and I used our spikes to fight off any attackers that got too close. The hallway was somewhat clear. An attacker presented himself once in a while, but for the most part we rushed up the sloping hall. Behind us the enemy roared their battle cries as they pursued us. We moved for what seemed like an eternity. Then we came to another open room. On the far side waited another small army of enemies. It was the first time I got a good look at them. They were all very broad-shouldered with huge barrel-like chests. Their forearms were quite large and they all had scruffy faces and wore strange spectacles. They stood in battle formation, waiting for us to move upon them. Behind us we could hear many more of the enemy coming up the hallway. We were trapped! There was only one way to get out of this situation. Custos yelled "charge!" and we all moved forward, pushing against the enemy in their center, trying to break their lines in order to get to the door that was behind them.

Custos and Omnus cut down the enemy in front of us like flies. Kibal seemed to be helping the two front men, so I moved to the back to help Mendax and Procul, as the enemy who had been pursuing us down the hall started to spill in through the doorway behind us. One of them threw his spike immediately upon entering the room. It flew straight and true, nailing Procul right in the chest. The man let out a great yell and moved back to attack the advancing enemy. He yelled "go" to us as we attempted to pull him back to the group.

As this was happening Custos broke through to the door and yelled at us to make a dash. I ran out the door and up the slope with Ms. Peranio, the boy and Grant. Custos stepped back into the action, but by this time the fighting was too intense. Omnus had been engulfed and Kibal was doing his best to free him. They both were taken down by the enemy. I gaped in horror as they stabbed Omnus over and over again. The enemy stepped back and I could not believe my eyes, but I saw Omnus slowly melting away. I had no time to question what I had just seen; I was in survival mode. Custos grabbed Mendax and they scampered up the hallway behind our group. Luckily for us we did not meet any more of those strange warriors on our way to the top of the hall. When we got to the end of it we saw that another heavy stone door barred our path. We all pushed against it, but to no avail. Then Mendax and Custos showed up, and we all forced the doors open and spewed back out into the driving rain. By this time my lungs were on fire, but we had no choice other than to keep running. We ran into the jungle, tripping and stumbling through the underbrush to get back to the road. Once we found the road we flew down the path and back out into the uninhabited rainforest. We did not know if those men or whatever they were, were following us or not. We did not wish to stick around and find out either.

We made it to the end of the road as it became pitch black, the lightning still lighting our path once in a while as we continued to cut into the jungle. Custos by now had taken the lead and was pushing us ahead. Grant followed behind him with Ms. Peranio next. I made sure the boy could keep up with me and Mendax brought up the rear. He still had both of his swords in his hands. He was bleeding heavily from a wound in his arm. About a mile into the jungle we stopped for the night. We hunkered down in a low-lying patch of bushes. We were all panting heavily. Custos ripped off a piece of cloth from the leg of his pants and gave it to me. I then tied it tightly around Mendax's arm above the gruesome cut. He looked quite pale from what I assumed to be the loss of blood. We could not sleep that night; we thought every sound we heard might be the enemy closing in around us. I was lying next to Mattie; she had not moved all night long. But when I did happen to catch a look at her face in the quick white light of a lightning bolt, I noticed that her eyes were wide open, staring up into the canopy. She had witnessed too much that day, and I felt certain she was in shock. The horrible part was I could do nothing to help her.

Brighton Bay Sanitarium
Assistant Warden Achiel Caldwell's Log
May 5, 1949

It was early the next morning when Custos got us up and moving again. He did not look well at all. His skin seemed pale and he was moving slower than usual. Mendax appeared to be on death's door. During the night, Custos had bandaged his arm and the bleeding had stopped, but beyond that the wound seemed to be no better. We had to go at a much slower pace this time, because the boy was too exhausted and Ms. Peranio was in a zombie-like state of shock. We were trying desperately to find the second rock, and thus our trail back through the forbidden part of the jungle and out into Q'eqchi land.

We discovered the second rock around midday. Custos spotted the top of it to our left as we trudged through the jungle. We got back on our path and easily made our way to the first rock and beyond into Q'eqchi land. When we reached the edge of the forbidden forest and the beginning of Q'eqchi land, I for some reason noticed that the landscape seemed to change. Q'eqchi land looked so much more manicured and less dense, as if every plant had been trimmed back to just the right size. It was very strange to me how my perspective of this part of jungle had changed dramatically after entering the forbidden terrain. We easily made our way into Q'eqchi land. It had been cloudy all day, but as we got further away from the forbidden lands, we noticed how the clouds started to break up and just as the sun was setting, it sent its rays down upon us like the embrace of a mother's hug. Custos stopped suddenly as the sun rays hit him. He opened his arms wide as if welcoming as much of the sun's rays as he could. It was the first sunlight we had seen since entering the forbidden territory.

That night we lit a tiny fire and Custos, Grant, the boy, and I began to formulate a plan about how to get back to the city of Tulum to radio Pista that we had failed and to wait for further instruction. The big problem we would face now was the lack of food. Up till now we had gotten all the fresh water we could possibly want because of all the rain. But food had been scarce and what with us running for our lives, we were suffering from very low energy. We were going to have to slow our pace and get food before we could continue.

Another issue was that we now had no way of communicating with the boy who was our only source of help in this situation. I tried my best to use gestures and draw in the dirt to talk to him, but he simply could not understand. I was about to give up when he touched my arm and I heard him say, "What do you need of me, master?" I turned around quickly and stared him right in the face. He looked startled.

"Custos, did you hear that? The boy spoke in perfect English!" Custos looked at me as if I was crazy. "He didn't say a word you fool," Grant exploded as he lounged on a log across from me. "I swear I heard him," I said, looking deeper into his eyes.

"Say it again, boy." But the boy did not speak. I pondered what had just happened. Maybe I was going crazy. We bedded down early and decided not to have a watch in order to try to recover what strength we had left.

Brighton Bay Sanitarium
Assistant Warden Achiel Caldwell's Log
May 6, 1949

This day was spent foraging for food. We found nothing and did not move far from where we camped. I fear that if we do not get food or water by tomorrow, Mendax will die and the rest of us are not far behind. My stomach aches right now as I write this. I am growing very weak and tired. This is all I can manage to write today.

Brighton Bay Sanitarium
Assistant Warden Achiel Caldwell's Log
May 7, 1949

Today started out how yesterday ended. We all seemed capable of nothing more than lying around camp. Even Custos could not find the energy to get up and try to hunt for food. By mid-afternoon we had all given up on living and accepted that this was how we would meet our end.

Mendax grasped to the edge of life. He panted heavily and was lost in a deep fever. His arm had begun to turn a nasty green color from the wound, and it had a disgusting odor. Around mid-afternoon we heard something rustling about in the jungle beyond us. We thought it might be the enemies who had finally caught up to us and were about to easily dispatch us into the afterlife. Instead a large native burst onto our path. He looked at us and began to call to someone behind him. Two more figures came into sight, and I heard one of them say, "Good Lord in heaven!" as he took a look at our sorry company. That was when I realized it was Dr. Toepfer, Seneca, and Manus They quickly dispensed water and food to all of us. Dr. Toepfer then went to work on Mendax "The arm is beyond repair; we are going to have to amputate it" he said. Seneca collected wood for the fire, while Manus kept passing out food and water to bring the rest of us back to our senses.

We made a large fire, and Manus offered up his sword to use in the procedure. Manus put his sword deep within the coals of the fire and let it sit for some time. The sun was starting to disappear when Dr. Toepfer took the sword out of the coals. It was almost shimmering with a bright orange and fiery red color. He had Seneca and Manus hold the delirious man, while he raised the sword over his head and brought it down. The cut was precise and clean. The arm fell straight to the ground. It was quite a gruesome sight. The doctor took the hot sword and placed it on the stump of Mendax's arm. You could hear the flesh sizzle and see the smoke rising, which left all of us gagging and trying to cover our mouths.

The most astonishing part of the whole procedure is when I looked down at the decrepit, severed arm on the ground, it was melting - literally melting! The flesh was spilling away. A puddle of white cream was all that was left after a few minutes. We all took notice of the phenomenon. Dr. Toepfer looked at Custos for some sort of explanation, but Custos seemed to play it off like it wasn't a big deal. That night I was able to get up and move on my shaky legs again. It hurt at first, but I felt it necessary to attempt some sort of exercise to get the blood pumping again. After moving about the camp for a few minutes, I began to think about Mattie. I hoped she would recover from the shock she was suffering from; if anyone could understand what she was going through it would be me. I lie down and fell instantly into a dreamless sleep.

Brighton Bay Sanitarium
Assistant Warden Achiel Caldwell's Log
May 8, 1949

Our group was beginning to show signs of life again. Even Mendax's fever broke today. Dr. Toepfer hoped that by tomorrow Mendax would come out of his coma. Ms. Peranio, Grant and the boy all seemed to be getting up and around, but Ms. Peranio still seemed distant. She stared off into space and would not make eye contact with anyone. I asked the doctor if he had any more chocolate left. He gave me a piece and I went over to sit next to Mattie. I took her hand in mine in order to make her aware of my presence.

She spoke softly to me. "What do we do now, Ace; where do we go from here?" I looked straight ahead as I held her hand. "I think we get out of this jungle and try to return to Brighton Bay. We need to get some semblance of normality back in our lives. We have to put these events behind us, bury them deep, where they can't haunt us anymore. It will take time, but perhaps together you and I can work towards that end."

I looked over at her, and she was staring straight at me with a look of astonishment on her face. I immediately let go of her hand, "What?" I said. "I never said anything; it was as if you read my thoughts. How could you have known what I was thinking?" Now it was my turn to try to play something off.

"I definitely heard you ask me a question. Perhaps you didn't realize that you had spoken." I gave the chocolate to her and quickly walked away. I did not know what was going on, but I could sense that something had changed. This was the second instance where I thought someone had spoken to me but nothing had been said. I tried to piece together the two occasions in order to understand what had happened. The only thing I could think of was that there had been physical contact both times. I decided to try an experiment.

I went over to Grant and grabbed his shoulder, "Hey, Grant, how are you doing? Are you feeling okay after our big ordeal?" I waited a second as I looked at him.

"Why is this idiot talking to me? Isn't it enough that everyone views him as this great leader? Now he has to come after me?" I instantly took my hand off his shoulder as he spouted off how he was fine. I simply shook my head and walked away. I couldn't believe it! His mouth had not moved the entire time I was hearing him; he simply stared at me and shook his head. That was it; I understood now, somehow I had received the power to hear inner thoughts.

Brighton Bay Sanitarium
Assistant Warden Achiel Caldwell's Log
May 9, 1949

Today we began to move again. Seneca and Manus made a stretcher for Mendax. The boy and Seneca led the way, while Grant and I helped Manus carry Mendax. Dr. Toepfer helped Ms. Peranio and whichever one of us was not helping carry Mendax took the rear position. We made it about eight miles by sundown. We decided to keep going as Seneca said that the boy had explained we were very close to the edge of Q'eqchi territory. At about 11:00 p.m. we stopped at what Seneca said was the outer rim of the boy's terrain that he knew. Seneca seemed to think that if we could keep to hunting trails, we had about three days of travel left before we could come to the city of Tulum. The problem was that we would be entering enemy tribe territory once again. We made camp and decided to sleep in rather late the next morning, because we knew we would have to take turns on watch the next few nights.

Brighton Bay Sanitarium
Assistant Warden Achiel Caldwell's Log
May 10, 1949

Today we made our way easily by moving on hunting trails, until we hit enemy territory around six o'clock in the evening. We decided to take the trail and see where it would lead us. We followed it even after the sun went down, because we seemed to be making good time. We moved slowly after the sun went down until about ten o'clock.

As we were setting up camp a few of us heard a loud rustling noise in some of the bushes near our camp. Custos and I went to search for the source of the sound. We were relieved to see a leopard sitting there with some sort of small deer for his late dinner. I had the early morning watch, and although the boy got up to watch with me, I felt alone and afraid - as if there were thousands of eyes watching my every move ready to pounce on me.

Brighton Bay Sanitarium
Assistant Warden Achiel Caldwell's Log
May 11, 1949

We moved slower today; you could really tell that Seneca's wounds were still bothering him. He seemed sluggish and out of breath. The spear wounds in his stomach became enflamed, and one even began to bleed. Mendax seemed to have come around a bit. I saw him talking to Manus once or twice. More than once during our hike I thought I saw smoke rising somewhere in the east. I hoped that it was a fire from the town of Tulum.

That night we had the late watch and as I sat there with the boy, I began to think about being able to read minds. I figured I would try it again. I clasped the boy on the shoulder and looked into his eyes. "Yes, master?" I heard. I decided to try something different "What is your name?" I thought in my mind as I looked at him. His eyes got very big, as if he were afraid. I tried to give him a reassuring look and asked him the question again. Then after a moment he answered "My name is Juwasimet." It was my turn to be astonished. The boy had understood my question! He could not only hear me, but my question had also been translated into his native tongue. This strange gift I had somehow found in the jungle was not only the ability to read minds, but also to cross language barriers with ease. I considered my gift for a while; it would probably be wise to keep something like this to myself. I thought it might come in handy in the future.

Brighton Bay Sanitarium
Assistant Warden Achiel Caldwell's Log
May 12, 1949

We trudged along today without many issues. Seneca seemed better. His welts did not look so inflamed and he was not breathing as heavily. It began to rain in the afternoon, making the paths slippery. We kept walking, even after the grey turned to black. Dr. Toepfer had taken the lead, as he had our only compass. It was about 10:30 p.m. when the jungle seemed to melt away around us, and as we looked up we saw the amazing tiered palace of the ancient Mayan City of Muyil looming over us. We had made it out of the jungle! Walking another three miles, we came to the sleepy town of Tulum. We proceeded to stay on the outskirts of the town until we came to an old stable. Custos told us to take shelter here for the night, seeing as it was too late to find an inn. I thought it was strange that he would choose an old abandoned building, but being so fatigued I really didn't care where I could lay down. We plopped ourselves down onto hay. For the first time in over two weeks I was sleeping on something other than the hard ground. Needless to say I was asleep instantly.

Brighton Bay Sanitarium
Assistant Warden Achiel Caldwell's Log
May 13, 1949

I woke up late the next morning to someone knocking on the door to the stable. It was Custos, and I found out from him that today was extraction day. We were all headed back to Natavis to brief Pista on the events of our adventure. I thought it strange how he said we were all going to Natavis, but I was too excited to ask questions. I had come to Tulum with a large backpack full of supplies; now. I was leaving this place with only my wallet, the inscribed rock (I had gotten from the marketplace in Tulum) and my little green leather-bound book.

We ate a hardy breakfast at a restaurant close to the barn we had stayed in. I must have had like five plates of eggs and chorizo. We then went to the local air field to await the plane that was coming for us. I thought it strange how Seneca and Dr. Toepfer were brought without any questions or reservations. I figured both would want to get back to their normal lives. Neither of them seemed to mind too badly though. A small plane touched down at about 2:00 p.m., circling around and coming to a stop in front of us. Fortis jumped out and embraced Custos and Manus before going to talk with Mendax, who was still lying on a stretcher.

We all loaded into the small plane that never would have fit our entire party had they all survived. I took a minute to think about those we left behind as I sat on the plane and looked out the tiny window at the village and the jungle beyond. The pain of all their deaths was fresh on my conscience, but as we took off I told myself, *I must try to leave the gruesome scenes of their deaths behind in the enormous graveyard of the jungle. But what would I do with their memories? What exactly did they die for?* We did not find the grail and whoever those evil people were in the temple, stole Patronis from us. We were returning empty-handed; the mission had been a complete failure. I was at a loss for what to do next. Like Ms. Peranio had said, was this really the end of our adventure? Custos came to sit next to me, telling the boy to move to another seat. He looked fidgety and uneasy. He suddenly spoke in a whisper to me.

"You and your friends are headed for great peril."

I was not going to allow a comment like that to unnerve me. "I've heard that twice before. Were you the one trying to tell me?"

"I have no idea what you are talking about, but I need you to listen to me right now. When we get back to Natavis, Pista is going to kill you and your friends."

"What? He can't do that! We have people waiting for us back at the sanitarium. Dr. Ambridge is waiting for our return. Isn't it obvious that if we don't return, Pista would be the first to be suspect?"

"Pista set up all of your deaths. He sent word to Ambridge over two weeks ago. He was informed that you all died in the hotel fire before you went to look for Patronis. Pista even had bodies planted in the hotel in order to prove you died. You and your friends have seen how our world works; you all know too much."

I was shocked; I could not believe what I was hearing! I knew too much? Our world? I felt lost. After this journey I felt like I was not sure of anything anymore. Custos went on.

"You must tell Mr. Pista you are the Destrugo. He may save you then and use you for his purposes."

"Wait, why have I heard that word before?"

"It's used in *the Legends of Green Eagle's* to describe the one who has come to put an end to our way of life.

"What's all this 'our way of life' talk? Why would he care about this Destrugo character? It's a fictional character in a book full of legends."

"After all you have seen, after all that you experienced, you still do not believe? The book tells a story yes, but not the 'legends' most people believe. It is the historical account of my people, Achiel. Your life is in danger, because you have been exposed to our world."

"What do you mean your world, your people?" I was becoming angry now.

"I am an Insignem Soparli. Natavis is where one of the great sects of the Soparli lives. Draxman Pista is our leader. You may have thought your adventure was coming to an end, Achiel, but really it is only beginning."

Epilogue

The Legends of Green Eagle
Interpreted by: Benito Cajero
Told by: Ta'awa Hotsko
Calabre XII

There was a Syreni priest who lived near the bottom of the ocean, whose name was Verniamin, and while he knew many things, he had a great fascination with the ending of the earth. Verniamin wanted desperately to know how the great lines of the Semper Nefas (Strix, Syreni, Soparli and Sapator) would cease to exist. One day a great light shown down through the water and landed upon Verniamin. A thunderous voice boomed down upon him through the murky waters. "There shall come a day when your people will be no more. They shall be destroyed for their evil deeds. The Destrugo shall come and seek the sword Salis Panem. When he finds it he shall destroy all the Semper Nefas who stand against him. Only mankind can stop his quest for revenge against the beasts of this world. Beware the Destrugo." The light faded and the voice went quiet. Verniamin spent the rest of his life trying to discover the truth behind the epiphany. He wrote a small scroll explaining the findings. It was stored away at the bottom of the ocean like many other treasures that the world has forgotten. Someday, when the world is in its death throes, the scroll will become important once again. He who finds the scroll shall know the whereabouts of the Salis Panem.

Characters

Achiel Byron Caldwell: The main character who is sent on a mission to retrieve Gabriel Patronis

Gabriel Patronis: A Psych ward patient who escapes and is on the run chasing after what he calls "his quest"

Mattie Peranio: A nurse from Brighton Bay Sanitarium who accompanies Achiel to find Patronis

Dr. Edward Ambridge: Warden at Brighton Bay Sanitarium

Donald Grant: Guard at Brighton Bay Sanitarium, sent to help Dr. Caldwell retrieve Patronis

Mrs. Kettler: Head nurse at Brighton Bay Sanitarium

Mr. Trundle: Chief Guard at Brighton Bay Sanitarium

George Barden: Patient at Brighton Bay Sanitarium; murdered

Cooties Jones: Patient at Brighton Bay Sanitarium

Sarah Tralton: Patient at Brighton Bay Sanitarium

Mr. Jerry Benson: Policeman sent with the search party to find Patronis

Sheriff MacKenzie: Chief of Police in Brighton

Mickey: Owner of a local bookstore in Brighton

Draxman Pista: Wealthy eccentric who funds the journey to retrieve Mr. Patronis

Custos: Pista's bodyguard, sent to accompany Caldwell and protect him on the journey to find Patronis

Mendax: An employee of Pista, and a member of Patronis's search party

Manus: An employee of Pista, and a member of Patronis's search party

Omnus: An employee of Pista, and a member of Patronis's search party

Fortis: An employee of Pista, and a member of Patronis's search party

Dicere: An employee as Pista's messenger

Artibus: Personal physician to Draxman Pista

Dr. Heinrich Toepfer: German doctor sent with the search party into. Yucatán

Allan Abbitt: An archeologist, and scholar from Britain. Came to help the search party to find a long lost temple

Pierre Dubois: Navigator, who becomes the party's guide of the search party as they head into the Yucatán

Seneca: A warrior native who is brought along as a translator for the search party as they enter the Yucatán

Kibal: Native Mayan trailblazer for search party

Ikal: Native Mayan trailblazer for search party

Ixil people: Native Mexican people who are at war with the Q'eqchi people

Q'eqchi people: Peaceful Native Mexican tribe

Padre Benito Cajero: A monk who was sent onto Native American lands to build a church. He finds a man named Green Eagle and writes down fascinating stories that the old man tells. He later calls the script *The Legends of Green Eagle*.

Green Eagle: Old Hopi Tewa Native American who tells fantastic stories to the children in his village

People from *Legends of Green Eagle*

Quomvi Ta'aho: god-like figure; creator of the Semper Nefas

Dominebris: The main character in the Legends; well known for being the father of the Semper Nefas.

Sapator: Mole-like creature created by Quomvi Ta'aho to help Dominebris

Ensignem Soparli: Lizard-like creature created by Quomvi Ta'aho to help Dominebris

Syreni: Fish-like creature created by Quomvi Ta'aho to help Dominebris

Strix: Owl-like creature created by Quomvi Ta'aho to help Dominebris

Tangella: Queen mother of the Strix

Tapani: Leader of the Soparli; responsible for the death of Dominebris

Lien: Messenger sent from the Strix to talk to Tapani

The Incendit: Ten children taken from their own villages and made new in order to serve Dominebris

Vernaimin: Syreni priest who learned about the Destrugo

27913259R00117

Made in the USA
Columbia, SC
04 October 2018